A FIGHTIN' HOMBRE

Luke Starn was hell-bent on making a dishonest fortune in the shortest possible time. There was only one man who could stop him—Laredo's hard-riding quick-shooting deputy sheriff.

Books by Norman A. Lazenby
in the Linford Western Library:

SINGING LEAD
A FIGHTIN' HOMBRE

NORMAN A. LAZENBY

A FIGHTIN' HOMBRE

Complete and Unabridged

LINFORD
Leicester

First Linford Edition
published April 1990

British Library CIP Data

Lazenby, Norman A. (Norman Austin)
A fightin' hombre.—Large print ed.—
Linford western library
I. Title
813'.52[F]

ISBN 0-7089-6810-4

Published by
F. A. Thorpe (Publishing) Ltd.
Anstey, Leicestershire
Set by Rowland Phototypesetting Ltd.
Bury St. Edmunds, Suffolk
Printed and bound in Great Britain by
T. J. Press (Padstow) Ltd., Padstow, Cornwall

1

JED RYLAND raced his big roan over the semi-arid land. He urged the horse on towards the dried-up creek. The aroma of sage floated through the dust-laden air. A brassy sun had brought out sweat on rider and horse, and it streaked in rivulets through dust.

Jed rowelled the animal over the watercourse, and then headed up the slope to the clumps of juniper and sycamore. The roan, wide-eyed and snorting, gained the shelter of the trees. Jed Ryland rode hell-for-leather down the other side of the slope. Only after a mile had been sliced through did he ease the blowing horse. Then he smiled, patted the horse's neck. As the cayuse went on at a walk, Jed went through the pockets of his black shirt and got out the makings. He rolled the cigarette, lit with a match which he carefully extinguished. He pushed back his black

1

Stetson, fingered the dust round his yellow bandanna. He was grinning thinly.

He was a tall, hard-framed man. Firm lips were always ready to smile. He had intensely blue eyes and hair bleached blond by exposure to the sun. He was a rannigan of deft, swift movements. He wore two Colts in cutaway holsters, and the leather was shiny with use.

After the roan got back wind, he applied steel again. The horse went off at a canter, over the floor of the sage-covered valley. Jed Ryland was making for the broken country. The huge buttes rose from the valley bed less than four miles distant.

In the meantime, a posse of riders, headed by Sheriff Ezra Strang, had thundered over the arid land and came to the dried-up creek. But instead of climbing the slope, they urged horses along the direction of the creek. After three miles along the winding trail the posse pounded into El Centro.

The ramshackle town of tin shanties and adobe huts lay stinking in the sun.

2

Mexican children and chickens played in the alkali dust. A few vaqueros lounged on the boardwalk of a saloon or cantina. As Sheriff Ezra Strang stamped into the place, boots rasping on boards, the Mexicans exchanged glances and moved away.

Two posse-men came into the saloon with the sheriff. Ezra Strang's moustache was bristling with rage. He stared around the saloon, finally settled grim grey eyes on the sallow bartender.

"You, durn yuh! Where's that hombre who just rode in? Don't tell me he didn't ride in hyar! We burned good leather a-comin' after thet rannigan. Where is he?"

The bartender grinned.

"I ain't seen any feller ridin' special fast. Who yuh wantin' this time?"

"That galoot who come a-ridin' into El Centro just a bit ahead o' us. A feller in black shirt and hat. A straw-haired devil with blue eyes! Goes by the name o' Jed Ryland."

The bartender wiped the rough pine counter.

"Ain't see him. What's he done?"

"What's he done!" roared Sheriff Ezra Strang. "Why, thet durned polecat rode into Monument City and held up a bank —thet's what he done, damn him! Got away wi' a thousand dollars in bills. Ain't thet right, fellers?"

Sheriff Strang turned to the posse-men. They nodded and growled. They were walking warily around the saloon, staring out of the back windows. They had six-shooters in hands and looked as if they would use them pretty fast.

"Wal, thet hombre ain't bin in here!" snarled the bartender. "What d'you figger this is, anyway?"

"Lissen, hidin' men is the chief business of El Centro!" bawled the sheriff. "Some day I'm goin' tuh clean this pesky hole out. Right now I ain't got time. Let's go look for that robber. I'll nail his hide to a barn-door when I get him."

The sheriff and the posse-men stamped out to join the others in the lawless settlement. The bartender exchanged glances

4

with two lounging border rannigans. The men came up to the pine counter again and ordered red-eye.

El Palermo Saloon was the only one-story building in the outlaw town. At the base of the stairs a big dark-haired man suddenly appeared. He smiled at the bartender. It was a significant smile. Texas Callahan had heard everything the sheriff of Monument City had bawled out.

"This Jed Ryland seems kinda an interestin' gent," he drawled. "Mebbe some other hombre would like tuh know 'bout him, too. Yeah, mebbe."

He went to the counter and ordered a drink. He spent some minutes staring at the back mirror. Texas Callahan was an Irish-Mexican, a potent combination. He was a fast man in a fight, and he had clawed for hoglegs in many a gun duel.

Over in the heat-hazed valley, Jed Ryland cantered the roan steadily on.

He was thinking he'd have to meet up with some galoots pretty soon. He'd have to find the jiggers he was looking for. Because he could not go back to

Monument City. That town of cattlemen and respectable traders was not for him.

He reached the first of the towering buttes. He stared up at the red bluffs where wind and rain had scoured weird shapes out of the rock. It was lonely terrain, and he had seen no one. Only a herd of longhorns following a lead steer moved in the distance, and they were at least three miles away. It was empty, sweeping country out here.

He threw the roan's reins over its head and groundhitched the animal. He thought he would squat in the shade of an outcrop of rock. He got down and sat in the hot sand. He took out the makings once more and rolled a cigarette. Then, as he sat back, keen eyes scanned the arid valley before him.

Twenty minutes later he saw the black speck of a rider cantering easily across the land. Jed Ryland watched with narrow eyes. A serene smile still played on his lips. He just waited.

The distant rider came through the heat hazes towards the broken country. Jed

Ryland waited patiently, and then he rose, vaulted into the saddle. He rode the horse out from the rocks. The other rider saw him and changed direction slightly.

They met in the valley with the towering buttes as a background. Jed saw that the stranger was a big man with the dark eyes and hair that spoke of Mexican or Indian ancestry.

"Howdy, stranger," called Jed.

"Howdy," drawled the other, and his eyes flickered over Jed Ryland's black shirt and hat, saw the tufts of blond hair thick at the edges of the Stetson. "Yuh happen to be a hombre named Jed Ryland?"

"Maybe I've heard o' the name," admitted Jed. "Yuh got a reason fer askin'?"

"Yep. Bin a jigger name o' Sheriff Ezra Strang lookin' for this galoot. Seems this feller bust into a bank and got himself some dinero."

"Yeah?" said Jed Ryland.

"Yuh don't have to worry about me," laughed Texas Callahan. "I ain't working for Ezra Strang. I figgered I might find yuh out here somewheres. Yuh looking fer a contact, feller, thet pays better than lone-wolf work?"

"Could be?" admitted Jed. "But I'm a stranger to this territory. I ain't got no contacts so far. Mebbe I'll jest work alone."

"Thet wouldn't be wise, Ryland. There's a gent round these parts who don't like lone jiggers pickin' up loose dinero."

"Is that so? Who's this gent?"

"Feller name o' Krafton Webber. I work fer him.

"What's his business?"

"Anything with cash stickin' to it, feller. Krafton Webber runs an outfit that gits on to cattle or gold or any durn thing. Webber could do with some gunslingers."

"Thet's mighty interestin'. Where does this hombre hang out?"

"In the hills," said Texas Callahan, and he swept a gloved hand vaguely to the distant broken country.

"Yeah? Mebbe he's got some good grub, huh?"

"He gets some mighty good beef!" chuckled Texas Callahan. "He's kinda partickler about the beef, but he don't ever pay for it!"

"How'd I get to Webber?"

"Wal, I'm kinda headin' thet way myself."

"I'll string along with yuh, stranger. What's yore name?"

"Make it Texas Callahan. All right. Feed steel to yuh hoss. It's a fair ride to Krafton Webber's camp."

They rode through the heat of the day, taking a trail through the butte country. After some miles the rocky sentinels gave way to hills capped with game-filled brush, juniper and sycamore. Texas Callahan knew the trail all right. At times it was merely a deer track through scrub. The horses climbed and slithered over shale hills, turning through narrow ravines of rock. It was arid territory, and the home of the rattler. They were close to the Texas-Mexico border, and about a

9

hundred miles from the booming railroad town of Laredo.

"Does Webber live in the hills all the time?" asked Jed Ryland.

"Not durn likely. There's places like El Centro where a jigger can bet a bellyful and a game of faro."

"Howsabout Monument City?"

"Aw, thet's kinda hot!" growled Texas Callahan. "Thet doggone sheriff never lets up. Guess he'll taste lead any day."

"He was the jigger thet rode after me, huh?"

"Yeah. Only he figgered yuh had gone into El Centro. Mebbe yuh were lucky. He'd ha' strung yuh up with a rawhide noose iffen he'd got yuh."

But the serene smile did not drop from Jed Ryland's face at the thought of the ugly scene.

"Yuh got the dinero with yuh?" asked Texas Callahan suddenly, eyeing the other's belt and shirt pockets.

"Yeah. Why?"

"Krafton Webber will want a fifty split."

"Is that so? Hell, I got this dinero myself! What sort o' deal is this?"

"That's the way he operates. Fifty per cent for himself, an' the rest to the crew that does the work."

"I'll see Webber about this myself!" snarled Jed.

"Shore. Suit yoreself."

The trail led through a big area of woodland. Big cottonwoods grew in holes alongside rocky outcrops.

All at once a man was visible sitting on top of a big rocky pile-up. The man held a Winchester. Seeing Texas Callahan with the stranger, he did not make much play with the rifle. Instead, he bawled a greeting.

"Howdy, Texas! Yuh got yoreself a pard?"

"Yep. Webber still hyar?"

"Shore. Everybody's takin' it easy except me, dang it!"

The two rode into the camp. It was a clearing surrounded by rocky walls and thick trees. In the clearing were log huts and corrals for horses. One big shack stood apart from the others and was provided with a porch. On the porch two men sprawled in chairs. On a nearby table were bottles of whisky. One of the men was drunk, but the other just seemed to have drunk himself more morose and in-bitten.

"Thet's Krafton Webber," said Texas Callahan. "The drunk is Rowdy Karl, my side-kick. Me an' Rowdy manage lots o' things for Webber."

"Fer a share of the half Webber hands back?" grunted Jed Ryland.

The other narrowed his black eyes.

"Yeah. Webber's got brains, feller. He's an unusual jigger. He was once trained tuh be a lawyer, but I guess he had an outlaw streak. Now it's guns wi' him instead o' books!"

Krafton Webber straightened up when he saw the two riders. But Rowdy Karl just slouched in his seat and blinked drunkenly. Webber was not tall, but he had great breadth of shoulders. He was clean shaven, and his jowls were big and red. Rowdy Karl carried a week's black stubble on his chin. Webber wore a checked shirt, clean brown pants tucked into riding boots. Two holster belts criss-crossed from his waist, and the guns hung low on his thighs.

"All right—who's this feller?" Words slurred because of the drink, but the man's intelligence was still there.

"This jigger helped himself to some dinero in Monument City," said Texas Callahan. "He don't like Ezra Strang. He wants to join up wi' this outfit. That right, pal?"

Jed Ryland rubbed his chin.

"Right now I'd join in wi' anyone who can hand out some chow. I'm hungry!"

"We got the chow," grated Krafton Webber. "But hold on, hombre. I didn't git yore name?"

"Jed Ryland. Anythin' else?"

"Yep. Plenty. Where yuh come from?"

"Aw—bin ridin' for weeks. Left Arizona, if yuh want to know."

"I can tell a feller from Arizona." Webber nodded. "So yuh jest blew into

13

Monument and got some dinero. What sort o' dinero?"

"A thousand dollars!" drawled Jed Ryland.

"Fine. Hand over them bills."

"Do I have to pay to horn in on this outfit?" groused Jed Ryland.

"Hand them over, rannigan!" Krafton Webber's voice was menacing. "I'll show yuh how I operate."

Jed Ryland smiled softly as he put a hand inside his black shirt. He inserted lithe fingers into a pocket. He pulled out a wad of currency. He handed the green bills to Webber. He had to walk up the steps to the porch.

Krafton Webber examined them, counted them.

"A thousand dollars, shore enough. All right, Ryland, yuh workin' fer me. Yore cut is fifty per cent. Yore lucky seeing how yuh got this money alone. Yuh don't have to split with another waddy."

"Mebbe yuh got somethin' good to offer fer the five hundred dollars!" sneered Jed Ryland.

14

"We got something mighty good," said Webber softly, and he reached out for the bottle of whisky.

Rowdy Karl rasped boots on the porch and lurched to his feet. Something had got into his brain.

"Kin yuh sling them Colts, feller!" he sneered. "Gawd, I don't know why yuh want to rope another jigger into the play, Webber. Ain't we got plenty o' galoots?"

Krafton Webber's broad red face hardened.

"I'll decide on that!"

Rowdy Karl was a young fool who had ridden out of a good home. His mother and father worked hard on their poverty-stricken ranch on some poor land about fifty miles beyond Monument City. The life hadn't been good enough for the lusty young rannigan, and after getting into plenty of trouble and breaking his mother's heart, he had run away and joined up with Krafton Webber. In the last few months he had killed other men and helped rob stages and banks.

"Yuh're shore lucky, feller!" sneered

Rowdy Karl. "Yuh're horning in at a time when the outfit's all set for making a million."

"Glad tuh hear it!" said Jed Ryland dryly. "Any more details?"

"Shut yore trap, Karl!" snapped Krafton Webber.

The young rannigan realised his drunken tongue had slipped. He got pretty angry with himself and Jed Ryland. He took a sudden mad dislike to the other man. It was completely unreasonable, but on the frontiers violent-tempered men played with raw feelings.

"I don't figger yuh need this galoot!" he bawled. "Who the hell ses he's any good to us? Yuh're jest cuttin' a doggone stranger intuh big dinero!"

Jed Ryland figured he had to make a bold play.

As Rowdy Karl swayed on the porch beside him, Jed unbuckled his gun-belt. It was an invitation in itself, and the other man snarled his desire to fight.

Gun-belts dropped heavily to the porch

16

boards. Jed Ryland backed down the steps. Rowdy Karl pounded after him.

Krafton Webber raised a hand and waved warningly to Texas Callahan. It was a signal that no one had to interfere.

A rough-house was an entertainment. Magically, men appeared out of the other shacks, leaving duties such as cooking and grooming of horses. Soon about ten men were formed into a circle.

Jed Ryland rammed out a hefty right that pulsed with steam. Rowdy Karl felt the blow rasp past his head, nearly tearing his ear off. He had swayed just in time to dodge the blow. The young fellow's hat fell off and rolled in the dust. Jed Ryland grinned, kicked the hat derisively. His own he had thrown down beside his gunbelt on the porch.

Fury chased all the drink fuddle out of Rowdy Karl. He rammed out his first blows. A right and left hacked through air and landed on Jed's face. Muscles throbbed and stiffened. Simultaneously, he slammed shakers into the other's shirt. Rowdy Karl stumbled back. Jed followed up and planted two more at the man's jaw. It was like battering fists at a tree bole. Grimly, Jed waded in. He knew he could lick this youngster any time. He would hammer him now to settle the affair.

But Rowdy Karl had red-blooded manhood. Jed's blows shook him, but he curved two thudding hooks back at his man. Jed felt the pile-driving slams shake his whole body. He shook the momentary numbness out of his head. He threw punches back as if he was hurling rocks.

Rowdy Karl got too many frame-shaking thuds to the jaw while his own fists tried to stem the human pistons. He backed, stumbled and then backed some more. Jed Ryland finally got him against the rough boulder wall which was the foundation for the porch. Jed gritted his teeth, jaw clamped like an iron vice. He slammed wicked rights into the other's eyes. His left weaved at Rowdy Karl's arms, keeping them moving futilely.

Rowdy Karl's face was hammered first to the right and then to the left. Agony contorted the rannigan's face into a mask. Jed slogged a deliberate right into the body. The other doubled and air grated out of him. Jed planted the left into the jaw and straightened the in-bitten youngster. Rowdy Karl began to slide slowly down the boulder wall. As he slid, Jed Ryland knocked defeat into him. Solid, unceasing blows beat the hombre down. He tried to clutch at the rough wall for support. Jed Ryland rammed another punch that contorted the rannigan. Suddenly he lost grip and slumped. Jed stood over him. Rowdy Karl dragged at air, his head sunk in a daze. He was incapable of rising.

Plenty of laughs floated hoarsely from the assembled outlaws. The fight was over. They drifted back to the chores. Jed Ryland went back to the porch, picked up his hat and jammed it on. He gathered up his gun-belt and buckled it slowly; grim eyes flickered from Krafton Webber to Texas Callahan.

"Shore hope thet feller don't bear a grudge!" he drawled. "But I figger he

19

asked fer it. I either come into this outfit or I don't. Yuh kin decide, Mister Webber."

"I said yuh're in," snapped the outlaw. "Rowdy will forget this fight. Mebbe he had too much likker. '

"Mebbeso," observed Jed Ryland. "Wal, I'd like to eat an' I reckon my hoss could do with a rub down. When yuh want me, I'll be around."

Krafton Webber stopped him before he reached his horse.

"I figger I want yuh now. You an' Texas."

They both stared curiously.

"Shore, any time, Webber," drawled Texas Callahan. "What is it?"

"It's the big job," said Krafton Webber. "I'm goin' to ride in wi' you two hombres to Monument City to-night."

"The big job!" muttered Texas Callahan.

"Yep. You don't know it with being in El Centro all day, Texas, but I jest got word that Andrew Platt is ridin' into Monument jest before sundown."

"He ain't alone?" asked Texas.

"Thet old-timer is never alone when he comes back from them jaunts intuh the desert!" snapped Krafton Webber. "Yuh ought to know thet! Iffen my scout had located him afore, we'd ha' got after him. But thet old snakeroo never seems to be anywhere until he suddenly rides them burros o' his on tuh the trail leading into Monument."

"Yeah. The moment he gits sighted half the blamed town rides alongside him," sneered Texas Callahan. "They all want to know the same thing."

"Yeah. The same thing. But we'll git that hombre to-night. He won't be surrounded by folks all the durned time."

"Kin yuh tell me what this is all about?" asked Jed Ryland quietly. "Or is it a durned secret?"

Krafton Webber laughed loudly. Texas Callahan waited for his boss to speak.

"Shore yuh kin know about it, Ryland. Yuh're in on it. I like the way yuh work. Yuh're jest the hombre I need. Andrew Platt is an old galoot who knows where to

21

find a bonanza so big he c'd make the whole damned lot o' us rich in no time tuh mention. He ain't never filed claim on this gold mine, Ryland. He don't want anybody to know about it. He jest rides out into them desert hills with his string o' burros and comes back weeks later with plenty o' gold. No one kin ever locate him up in them desert hills. He allus shakes off any hombre who figgers tuh foller him."

"Plenty try thet," said Texas Callahan, his opaque eyes glinting. "I tried it once, the durned old snake! He jest lost me off!"

"Thet blamed sheriff, Ezra Strang, allus rides out wi' a posse to protect the old buzzard the moment the news gets to town thet Andrew Platt is coming back," said Krafton Webber.

"What's the set-up?" asked Jed Ryland. "Yuh gonna git some gold. But how?"

"We git Andrew Platt first," said Krafton Webber. He leaned forward in his chair, shrewdness on his vast face. Jed

Ryland knew the man could think ahead. "We want thet hombre up hyar. Then we make him talk. Jest to make shore he ain't foolin', we make him take us out to the bonanza after he talks. Then we'll be sittin' pretty. There's gold fer every jigger in this outfit. Thet's the plan. Git yore eats, Ryland, and look to yore hoss. We'll git to Monument fer sundown. Yore five hundred dollars is shore a good investment, hombre. But I'll need fellers like you afore we're through."

2

AN hour later Jed Ryland rode out with Krafton Webber and Texas Callahan. The other outlaws watched them go, and while some were envious, Rowdy Karl stared resentfully. His hatred of Jed Ryland had solidified into a real thing.

Jed Ryland was spruced up. His black shirt and hat had been cleaned of dust. His dark-coloured pants were tucked into boots that shone. Gloved hands held tightly to the roan's reins. Colts protruded from low on his hips. In his saddle holster was his rifle.

Webber had planned to hit Monument City just after sundown. They had to locate Andrew Platt and get him away.

"The way I figger it, the old coot will be holed-up in his house on the edge o' the town. He's got a tidy house with a fancy fence all around it an' flowers."

24

"A married hombre?" queried Jed Ryland.

"Hell, no! Thet old buzzard spent all his years ridin' a burro in the badlands lookin' fer gold. Nope, he lives alone. He'll ha' deposited his gold with the bank by now, I guess. Ef it weren't thet there's more gold in the bonanza, I'd git the men an' have a try fer the bank. But what he brought out is kinda chick-feed compared to what's lying in thet bonanza."

"Is it a rich strike the old feller's got?"

"Yep. Must be. Allowing fer the old jigger's doggone lying, there must be enough to make most o' Monument City rich. Andrew Platt takes a glass in the saloons, an' he sometimes gits to talkin'. He reckons he kin jest shovel the durned gold up—pure nuggets and gold-bearing quartz."

"How long's he bin getting gold out o' the bonanza?" asked Jed Ryland.

"About six months ago he brought the first load in. The doggone town went crazy. But the old gink keeps his trap tight about the location."

"Mighty dangerous secret tuh carry around. What the heck does he figger the claim office is for? Ef he filed claim, no one could jump the mine. Ef they did, the law would be behind Andrew Platt."

"Yuh're telling me!" drawled Krafton Webber dryly. "Shore is only a matter o' time afore some other rannigan gits the same idee as me. The old fool is askin' fer trouble, and he's gonna get it!"

Talk ceased on that, and the three riders rowelled the horses into a canter. The sun was glowing like a big red ball of fire. The arid land was streaked with beauty, but the three men were busy with their own thoughts. They had no time for the marvels of the towering buttes in the distance nor for the clumps of cholla cactus, ocotillo and a dozen other barbed desert growths. Miles away, out by Monument City, the grasslands began and here the ranchers grazed their herds of Texas longhorns. The lean, leery cattle had many thousands upon thousands of acres of gamma grass, and even in the semi-arid lands there was bunch grass and

26

other hardy grasses almost as nutritious as corn. The trouble with the longhorn was that he lost as much fat moving around for feed as the feeding gave him. But the cattle were hardy critters.

Slowly the three riders came down from the broken country and cantered along the vast valley that led to Monument City. There was no railroad at the town. Stages ran overland to Laredo, and freight went by wagon. There was always talk of the railroad pushing on to Monument City, but that was as far as it got.

By now the sun had sunk low on the horizon. In another few minutes the sun would sink its rays altogether. Nightfall came swift in the west.

"Remember," growled Krafton Webber suddenly, "I don't want this old hellion hurt. He ain't no doggone good dead. An' he is better kept in one piece. I've got to make him talk an' then ride out intuh the desert after thet mine o' his. Yes, sir, I want him plenty healthy!"

As they approached Monument City, lights began to glow. Viewed from across the sage-covered prairie, the lights were small winking pin-points. The lights came mostly from saloons and the lanterns hung at important points in the town's streets. Citizens usually fastened the shutters on their houses.

Krafton Webber and Texas Callahan knew where to find the old gold-mine owner's house. Jed Ryland did not know the location. But it did not matter. Hats low down over their eyes, the three men rode into the town. The dark shadows of the hard-earth streets were the best thing for the wanted men. They avoided the street corner lanterns and the pools of yellow light emerging above the batwing doors of the many saloons. The three riders passed other men in the streets with confidence. They would only be recognised as outlaws if they came face to face with an ex-posse-man or someone who knew them.

Eventually they arrived at a house set off the road on the east side of the town. Jed Ryland saw the nodding heads of tall flowers above a garden fence. This was

Andrew Platt's home. It was surprising to imagine a gold-mine owner living so modestly. But by all accounts, the old fellow was a queer one.

Krafton Webber was the first to dismount. He led his horse to a nearby tie-rail.

"Hitch yore hosses hyar," he muttered. "This ain't so near to the old jigger's house. We don't want to attract attention. All right. Let's see if the old hellion's at home."

Three big men walked steadily to the picket fence. Texas Callahan opened the gate. With only a slight sound from their boots, the three walked up to the clapboard house. But they did not knock on the door.

Texas Callahan crept silently around to the back of the place. Krafton Webber tried to see if there was a chink in the wood shutters which barred the windows, but there was none. Jed Ryland stood silently, awaiting orders. They came.

"Go git around to the stable at the back," hissed Krafton Webber. "Git the old coot's hoss saddled. Don't fail me, feller."

"D'yuh figger I'll fail?" returned Jed softly.

The other man patted his arm lightly.

Jed went down a path and quickly found the stable. He took out the wood wedge and opened the door. A horse whinnied softly, but hardly enough to be heard beyond the livery. Jed went in and found two horses. He chose a big bay, and soon spotted the rig it evidently wore. Working expertly he had the rig over the animal's head. Then he hoisted the saddle and tightened the cinch. Finally, he led the horse out carefully.

He dropped the reins when the horse stood in the darkness at the side of the house. Jed Ryland peered around. He could not see Krafton Webber, but yellow light slanted from the door.

He found the door slightly open and he walked in, hands hovering at hips.

Texas Callahan was grinning at an old-timer with grizzled white hair. Texas had a hand over the fellow's mouth, and another strong arm around the old man's body.

Krafton Webber held a big colt pointed at Andrew Platt's heart. Jed Ryland knew this play for bluff, but the old-timer could not be sure of that.

"Hoss all ready," lipped Jed Ryland.

"Mighty fine. Yep, it's mighty fine!" grunted Krafton Webber. "This old hellion answered the door with a gun in his blamed hand, but Texas got through the back door. He had tuh force the lock, but he walked up behind this old ranny and made him drop his durned gun."

"Easy so far," said Jed Ryland.

Krafton Webber spoke threateningly to the old-timer.

"Yuh're coming with us—get it? Jed, git some cloth and gag him. I figger this old hellion ain't got any respect for his own skin. Gag him an' tie him."

Jed Ryland looked around the house. He found an old bandanna in a closet. He bound it securely around Andrew Platt's head, covering his mouth. A coiled lariat hanging on the wall beside two ancient guns provided rope to bind the man's arms.

Andrew Platt glared with grim beady eyes. In the face of three determined men and a pointed colt, there was little he could do but submit.

He knew what the men wanted. As a matter of fact, he knew Krafton Webber from the wanted bills that decorated the outside of the sheriff's office.

The old fellow was led outside and propped up on his waiting horse.

The door of the house was closed carefully by Texas Callahan. They did not want some curious persons to arouse an immediate pursuit.

Krafton Webber led the bay out to the dark road himself. Swiftly, they came to the other three tied horses. The men leaped to the saddles. Andrew Platt balanced in his saddle, feet in the stirrups. He could not hold on to the saddle-horn. Jed Ryland had stuck the old-timer's hat on his head as he had left the house. It partly obscured the fact that Andrew Platt was gagged.

The four horsemen cantered down the dark road. There was no sudden gallop that would attract attention. They moved away from the centre of Monument City. They would circle the town from the outside and get on to the trail that led into the hills.

It happened they went past the sheriff's office, which lay on the edge of the town, law and order being one of the last things to arrive at Monument City. The town, like all western cow-towns, had had a turbulent past and still saw its share of bad men.

Neither Krafton Webber nor Texas Callahan knew how it happened, but without warning the horse carrying Andrew Platt suddenly whinnied and sprang forward in a frightened leap. The old man was nearly unseated, but he kept on by sheer expert horsemanship. His legs gripped to the animal's sides. The bay, snorting in sudden, mysterious fright, began crow-hopping. The other three horses wheeled away from the spooked animal. Krafton Webber cursed.

"What'n hell got into thet critter?"

Texas Callahan attempted to sidle his horse up to the frightened bay. But the animal was still imitating a rodeo bronc.

From out of the darkness between two store buildings a colt exploded. Flame lanced the night air.

Krafton Webber's horse reared in sudden fright. A loud neigh from the cayuse rent the air. Krafton Webber felt a slug tear into his shoulder. His cursing became one of pain.

Texas Callahan clawed for a gun and pumped a shell into the darkness between the stores.

At the same moment his horse was jerking in fright. He could not aim, and although born and bred to a saddle, he had plenty of work in checking his horse.

Then the colt from the darkness roared again. The heavy slug tore Texas Callahan's hat from his head and startled his horse afresh. Despite a tight rein, the horse leaped forward and thundered down the road.

Krafton Webber's horse, from the same

remuda, sprang after the other animal. In seconds the whole scene had changed. Andrew Platt, on his spooked horse, was somewhere in the darkness of the street. He could not be rounded up for men were appearing on the broadwalks. Light glowed from the door of the sheriff's office.

Krafton Webber's horse pounded out of the town, and the rider gave the animal its head. The owl-hoot boss knew it would not be healthy to ride back looking for Andrew Platt. Anyway, the wily old-timer would be sure to take advantage of the confusion. He'd get off his horse at the first chance and run for safety, even if his arms were bound.

Krafton Webber could not see his side-kick, Texas Callahan. The other's horse had galloped off into the darkness. Maybe Jed Ryland was feeding steel to get out of town, too.

Some hellion had shot at them from out of the dark street. Cursing, crouching over his cayuse, Krafton Webber wondered what exactly had happened.

What had startled Andrew Platt's horse? Had the old galoot kicked at the animal's flanks himself and started the shindig? That could be.

Pain in Krafton Webber's shoulder became intense. It was like a red-hot object burning constantly in the flesh. Blood was seeping down his arm, inside his shirt sleeve. He cursed more violently. He'd have to get the durned bullet dug out and the wound bandaged.

He kept the horse to the trail leading over the sage-covered land. Maybe the other two were ahead, or maybe they were behind. He figured to reach the broken country before he stopped in the hope that they would overtake him.

It was an hour later when he halted his cayuse. He sat in the saddle in the gloom of a towering butte. A moon was beginning to rise behind wispy clouds. Krafton Webber kept to the saddle because he knew he would have a hard task getting back to leather with an injured shoulder. Had he been all right, he would have dismounted and placed his ear to the ground. In this manner he would have heard any approaching hoof-beats. But he had to sit and hope that Texas Callahan or Jed Ryland were coming along.

He pulled off his bandanna with his right hand and tried to stuff it inside his shirt to stem the bleeding from the wound in his left shoulder. Then he waited, a grim, savage man, brooding on the events of the night.

As he waited, slumped in the saddle, he heard the distant sound of a horse clop-clopping over shale. Then came the outlaw call—an owl hooting in the night. The rider came nearer. Krafton Webber made a return call.

A minute later Texas Callahan rode through the rocky land ahead and came up to Krafton Webber. He had actually been ahead on the trail and had ridden back, knowing the others might be coming up.

"Hyar, Texas!" growled Webber. "Help tie this durned bandanna round my shoulder. I stopped a blamed slug outa thet hombre's gun."

"Hell's snakes, thet's bad!" exclaimed the other.

He jigged his horse closer. He leaned forward and began to pull Krafton Webber's shirt back. The outlaw boss hissed at the pain in the movement. Texas Callahan got the bandanna and wrapped it tightly round the shoulder. No more could be done for the moment.

"Where'n hell's thet Ryland hombre?" growled Krafton Webber eventually. "Didn't he git outa town same as us?"

"I never saw the feller," said Texas. "Don't know what happened tuh him."

"Mebbe he took tuh some other trail in the dark," muttered Krafton Webber. "Ef he don't ride up soon, tarnation with him. He'll ha' tuh find the camp the best way he can. Ef he kin do it in the dark, he's darned quick at noting a trail."

Texas Callahan changed the subject.

"Some snakeroo recognised us in town, boss. Hell, I never saw the hombre. He musta bin sittin' pretty in the dark when we passed along wi' Andrew Platt."

Krafton Webber looked restlessly

through the night. The moon, rising higher, was throwing more light over the arid land.

"Thet hellion shot tuh kill, Texas. He hit me in the shoulder, but it was jest because my hoss was bucking like a wild 'un. He meant tuh kill. I wish I'd sighted thet feller."

"Thet jigger put a slug through my hat," snapped Texas Callahan. He fingered the thong under his chin. "I had the blamed thing fastened down or I'd be without a hat. I threw a slug back at the rannigan, but Gawd knows if I hit him!"

"I wonder who in tarnation it was?" muttered Krafton Webber, "Mebbe it was thet blamed trigger hombre, Ezra Strang."

"Wal, the shootin' started near his durned office," returned Texas Callahan.

"Hev yuh ever heard o' such doggone bad luck!" raged Krafton Webber. "We had thet old fool nicely hog-tied and then everythin' gits knocked fer a loop. Damn an' tarnation! We'll ha' tuh make the play all over again. I've got tuh git this wound

fixed afore we kin figger another plan. An'
thet old fool will be kinda leery. Whar
the heck's thet Ryland feller? Ain't he a-
comin' this way?"

The silence of the night gave no answer
to these questions, and, angrily, Krafton
Webber spurred his horse. The two men
started on the journey to the outlaw
camp.

"I guess Jed will turn up somehow,"
Texas Callahan concluded.

With a wounded man, there was only
one move to make. They were going back
to the camp in the hills.

Krafton Webber, conscious of the
effect this would make on his prestige,
was filled with grim, sullen anger. But he
had to get back, and he had to get attention. There was a bullet in his shoulder.
He thought he could feel it grating on the
bone. He was not sure how it would be
extracted. Thinking about it did not
improve his temper. He just cursed his
bad luck.

Some hours later the two men rode
through the narrow passages in the rocky

pile-up and entered the camp clearing. A guard challenged them, and let them pass on a signal.

Krafton Webber lurched down from his saddle. He handed the reins of his cayuse to a Mexican wrangler. As the two horses were led away to the livery, Krafton Webber staggered into his shack. He disdained any help from Texas Callahan, and that individual realised he had not to offer it.

The outlaw boss sat on his bunk and jerked his good hand.

"See what yuh kin do with this wound, segundo. Wash it, clean it—do something."

The other's black eyes flickered uncertainly.

"Shore, Webber, but I ain't no doc. How yuh figger to git thet slug out?"

Krafton Webber came to a decision. To some extent he owed his leadership over the gang of border ruffians because he could plan decisively.

"Yuh kin git a doc—to-morrow! Put a tight bandage on my doggone shoulder now. At sun-up take three hombres and ride out fer a doc. I don't care whar yuh git him, but bring the feller up hyar. Ef he don't want to come, yuh know mighty fine how to persuade him."

"Ain't it dangerous bringin' a stranger up hyar?"

"Mebbe!" grunted Krafton Webber. "Mebbe for the doc after I'm through wi' him!"

Texas Callahan started to make his boss as comfortable as possible. Men could be tough living, but a slug in the shoulder was no joke. The slug hurt Webber just as much as any other fellow in the world.

Some time later the men bedded down for the night. Texas Callahan shared the shack with Webber. Rowdy Karl and the others who had waited to see the arrival of Andrew Platt had to hit the hay. Only the guard kept watch. For those who rode the owl-hoot trail, there was always danger.

At early sun-up, Texas Callahan roused the wrangler and summoned three other men. He told them what was wanted of them.

"The boss wants you to git a doc—any sorta doc. He'll either come along peaceful or we kinda make him. I don't figger this is so easy, but we kin do it. Okay. Git some chow and then git to leather."

Rowdy Karl was due to ride out on the task. Texas Callahan had selected him because they were partners in ruffian affrays. The wrangler got the men's horses saddled and led out. The four men were in the saddle, beside the corral, when a horseman appeared through the narrow, rocky passage that gave access to the clearing. Under the bowing trees, the rider passed.

"Jed Ryland!" exclaimed Texas. "Whar in tarnation has he been all night?"

Rowdy Karl rubbed a hand over his stubble. Sheer slovenliness was responsible for his beard. His eyes glinted at the sight of Jed Ryland. Hate for the other welled afresh.

"Yep. Whar's he bin?" he grated.

Jed Ryland rode up and reined his horse.

"Howdy, partners. Yuh settin' off agin to git thet old galoot?"

"Not exactly," drawled Texas Callahan. "Whar yuh bin all night?"

"Couldn't find the blamed trail to this hideout," retorted Jed. "In the dark it ain't so easy to track up to this place. I nosed around plenty an' then bedded down wi' my back to a tree, awaitin' for sun-up."

"Webber got a slug in him," said Texas briefly. "We got orders to git a doc."

"Is he bad hit?" inquired Jed.

"Nope. But Webber figgers a doc is better fer gittin' a slug out a hombre's shoulder than some horn-handed rannigan. I reckon yuh'd better talk to Webber. We're a-goin'."

"Yep. Yuh'd better account for yore-self, Ryland." sneered Rowdy Karl promptly.

"What the heck d'yuh mean by thet, podner?" asked Jed steadily.

"Did you stop any lead last night?" insinuated the other.

"Can't say I did."

"Texas tells me it was a mighty queer rumpus last night. That right, Texas."

The Irish-Mexican exchanged glances with Rowdy Karl.

"Yep. Guess it was. Some jigger took shots at us. First, somethin' startled Andrew Platt's hoss. Everything went kinda haywire after that. We lost the old-timer. My hoss got spooked with the gun explosions and jest used its laigs. Same thing with Webber—and Jed, I guess."

Rowdy Karl glowered at the blue-eyed man with the straw-coloured hair. He was hesitating, unsure. But he hated, all right.

"Yep, mighty queer, Texas. Mighty queer. Seems yuh had doggone bad luck. Wal, I guess we kin try agin. Ain't nuthin' thet says we can't! Mebbe Jed won't be in the party next time. Mebbe we'll have better luck!"

Jed Ryland sat stiffly in the saddle, blue eyes amused, a twist to his firm mouth.

His hands were restful and near to the saddle-horn.

The owl-hoot hombres knew a gun-man when they saw one. They also knew there was plenty of animosity between Rowdy Karl and the newcomer to the outfit. They didn't see much sense in the hostility.

"Will you two jest forgit it?" snapped Texas Callahan. "We ain't got all day to sit yapping. Feed steel to thet hoss, Rowdy. We got to git a doc for Webber. How'd yuh like to have a chunk of lead in yore shoulder? Adios, Ryland. Jest go to Webber. '

The party rode single file into the narrow passage between the rocks. The leafy foliage overhead hid them in seconds.

Jed Ryland led his horse to the livery, handed it over to the Mex wrangler. Then he made for Webber's shack.

3

"**S**O yuh didn't see that shootin' hombre last night?" muttered Krafton Webber.

He was lying back on his bunk. He was fully dressed, and inside his shirt his shoulder was freshly bandaged. But he had lost a lot of blood, and the wound throbbed.

"I was jest behind," said Jed Ryland. "Thet old hellion's hoss raised on its laigs and shore spooked my critter. I was tightening rein when thet hombre fired."

"Thet jigger meant to kill," snapped Webber, his eyes glittering with a spurt of anger. "It wasn't his fault he plugged my shoulder and not my blamed heart. Same wi' Texas. He got a hole in his hat. Might ha' bin his head."

"Seems a good thing the hosses got spooked," drawled Jed Ryland.

47

"Mebbe. How come yuh didn't catch up on the trail last night?"

"Guess I got on the wrong track. Then when I hit the broken territory, it was worse. I'm a stranger to these parts, Webber."

"Yeah. Wal, yuh'll have to git acquainted with the land. This set-back is only temporary. I'm goin' after thet old buzzard soon as this wound heals."

"Texas is away tuh git a doc?" queried Jed.

"Yep. Thar's two docs in Monument. One will do for me."

"What happens to the doc when he gits his sights on this camp? Yuh goin' to send him back to Monument and have thet doggone sheriff up hyar in no time?"

"Not durned likely," said Krafton Webber evilly. "If the doc fixes me, three things might happen."

"What's thet?" inquired Jed Ryland.

"Wal, hombre, this kinda unlucky doc can agree tuh being run outa the state or he kin stay hyar. If he don't like either, a bullet will fix him fast."

"I git it," said Jed.

He left Webber's shack and reflected that the doc who was brought up to the outlaw camp was taking a sure path to sudden death. Because Krafton Webber really meant a bullet for the man when he had served his purpose.

For Jed Ryland there were a few hours of waiting which he spent attending to his roan. He cleaned and rubbed down the cayuse. He examined the saddle rig. Then he had chow with the other owl-hoots in a rough bunkhouse. Rough and ready, like an outfit of cowpokes on a ranch, they accepted him for what he was worth. But there was a difference. These men were border ruffians of the worst type. Most of them would have killed their own kith and kin for a dollar. Some of the men were half-breeds, and there were two pure Mexicans. They wore the steeple-shaped hats of their kind and braided jackets.

Jed Ryland walked around the camp and noted how it was hidden by rocks and thick clumps of trees and scrub. He saw there were only two ways in or out of the camp. So far he was familiar with only one. He noted the position of the camp in comparison to the distant, tall hills.

And then there were sudden cries and greetings. Jed Ryland walked back swiftly to the shacks. He saw Texas Callahan ride through the narrow crack between the rocks. Then came one of the outlaws. Jed waited, wondering when the doc would appear.

But Rowdy Karl rode through next in the single file—and riding double with him was a girl.

She had evidently exhausted herself temporarily with struggles, for she sat stiffly in front of the young rannigan. She stared defiantly at the grinning gang. She was a girl with amazing red hair and fine, lovely eyes and mouth. She was clad in a buckskin skirt and jacket under which was a red checked shirt. Rowdy Karl had thrust her callously across the saddle and her skirts were drawn up almost to her knees.

As Rowdy Karl rode his horse in,

another rider appeared through the cleft. He, too, carried a passenger, but this time it was an elderly man with pale face and white hair.

Jed Ryland realised that this man was probably the doc, but who was the girl and why had she been brought to the outlaw camp?

The four riders of the owl-hoot trail trotted the horses up to the corral and then dismounted. Rowdy Karl swung the girl to the ground. He held her waist, and when her feet touched the earth he continued to hold her and grin unpleasantly.

"Say, Rowdy, did thar boss tell yuh to collect a wumman?" jibed a man.

"Nope!" bawled Rowdy Karl. "But this gal was with the doc when we sighted 'em ridin' a caravan into Monument. This gent is a travelling doc. We had to leave their goshdarned caravan out in the badlands, but we made the doc bring any amount o' medicine and gear. Yes, sirree, he's got everythin'. Yuh should ha' seen his caravan wi' two hosses. Ses on the side

51

o' the caravan, 'Doc Marsh Cures All Complaints. Teeth Drawn. Fevers Cured. Ointments For All Skin Troubles.' Wal, I guess the doc can fix the boss!"

There was a bawl of laughter at Rowdy Karl's words. Doc Marsh stood stiffly where he was placed. The girl struggled against Rowdy Karl's grip.

"Say, who's the gal?" called a man.

"The old doc says this is his daughter Jean!" guffawed Rowdy Karl. "Wal, now, Jean, what about a kiss?"

Jed Ryland walked slowly but steadily towards the group.

"Mebbe she don't want tuh kiss yore dirty pan, Rowdy," he said suddenly in a soft drawl.

The laughter ceased all at once. Only the residue of a few laughs lingered on. Jed Ryland walked through two men and shouldered up to Rowdy Karl. Jed fumbled in his shirt pocket and brought out paper and tobacco. He rolled the brown paper cigarette and stuck it in his mouth.

Rowdy Karl took his arms away from

the girl. But he did it only to square up to Jed Ryland.

"Yuh figger to git under my skin, hombre!" he snarled. "Wal, let me tell yuh—"

He got no further. A Colt roared through the air. Men ducked and scattered.

Krafton Webber stood on the porch of his shack gun in his right hand. His feet were squarely apart.

"When you rannigans are done yappin' mebbe yuh'll bring thet doc up hyar!" he roared. "For Gawd's sake, do I have tuh run everythin' in this outfit? Bring thet doc up hyar! He's got work to do!"

The interruption broke up the knot of men. Rowdy Karl, as one of Webber's chief side-kicks, gave an order for the girl to be led to a shack and locked up. Then the young rannigan hurried after Texas Callahan as Doc Marsh was led to Webber's shack.

Krafton Webber lay back on his bunk with a few grimaces of pain. Texas, Rowdy, Doc Marsh and Jed Ryland stood around the bare room. The movement did not improve Webber's temper.

"Why the devil did yuh bring thet gal hyar?"

"She was hell-bent on making trouble," rapped Rowdy Karl. "She tried to git a rifle offen the caravan. I stopped thet play an' then she said she'd git the sheriff of Monument City to ride out after us. So I figured it weren't no difference to bring two up hyar instead o' one."

"Yuh could ha' shut her up wi' yore gun!"

"I figured thet would make the old doc sore," argued Rowdy Karl. "He could trick yuh, boss. Yuh don't want to be watching him all the time. Anyway, yuh figger to set him back again after he takes thet bullet outa yore shoulder. Ain't thet right, Webber?"

And Rowdy Karl looked meaningly at the outlaw boss.

"Yep. Shore. Shore. Fix me up an' yuh kin git outa hyar wi' a whole skin, doc," grunted Krafton Webber.

Doc Marsh glared around him. He was

stoutish and wore a store suit and fawn hat. His pants were tucked into riding boots. He had a black tie properly tied with a white collar.

"You're a bunch of outlaws, I'll guess! I've bin told what I've got to do. All right, I'll take the bullet out. Jest set my daughter free—now, pronto."

"Yuh'll git set on the trail again when the slug's outa my shoulder," grunted Webber.

Doc Marsh drew himself up.

"I don't trust you. I don't know who you are—I'm a stranger travelling these parts—but I don't trust you, sir. Set my daughter free now and I'll perform any operation you need. Get Jean back to our caravan. I—I—put all my money into that outfit."

Anger, pain and exasperation chased over Krafton Webber's big, heavy face.

"All right. Rowdy, see to it. Git thet gal outa hyar. Take her back to the caravan. I don't know why yuh're so het up, doc. All I want is a slug taken out.

Then you an' your gal can git on yore way."

"I must protect my daughter, sir," retorted the oldster. "She's all I have. If I know she is safe—"

"Shore, shore. Now git on wi' it. Git this durned slug out. You, Rowdy, git thet gal back to the caravan."

Krafton Webber's eyes met Rowdy Karl's for a moment. In a second of invisible contact, the young rannigan knew his orders. No one else had seen the flashing glance.

Rowdy Karl knew he had to see that Jean Marsh did not return to Monument City with tales of the camp and how her father was taken there.

True to his word, Doc Marsh would not start until he saw his daughter. She was led out of the shack. A horse was brought out for her. The pretence was good enough until Doc Marsh saw Rowdy Karl get to his saddle.

"I want Jean to ride out alone," said the doc harshly.

Krafton Webber lurched out of the shack and on to the porch.

"Goshdarn it, let the gal ride out!"

Rowdy Karl knew the tone of Webber's voice, and he read his message. The order was still there. He had to get after the girl later. She would gain a head start, but he knew the land.

Doc Marsh waved to Jean as she rode out.

"Adios, my child. I'll join you soon. Don't worry about me. Just get to the caravan and ride to Monument City."

The girl waved helplessly. She had plenty of spirit, judging by the proud way she rode the horse, but there was precious little she could do.

"Father, I don't want to go without you! I don't trust—"

"Please go while you have the chance!" he interposed harshly. "Just trust in God, daughter!"

She jigged the horse forward at that and rode into the cleft. Doc Marsh did not move. Krafton Webber lurched back to his bunk and lay down. He was cursing, and his thoughts regarding Doc Marsh were not pleasant. But for the moment he needed the medical man.

Finally, Doc Marsh judged he had to move. Texas Callahan held a gun at him menacingly.

"Git goin', doc. The boss is waitin'. Yore gal is safe away now."

But as Doc Marsh turned and walked slowly into the shack, Rowdy Karl leaped to his horse and urged it towards the narrow passage in the rocks.

Jed Ryland watched him go, grim lines etched in his firm lean face.

Rowdy Karl had to gain on the girl. He jigged his horse through the narrow cleft between rocks and then rowelled the animal into a dangerous canter through the twisting trail, through the rocky pile-up. A few minutes later, clear of the outcrops, he forced the horse down a slithering shale slope. It was a short cut to the trail below. He knew he would sight the girl as she picked her way uncertainly to open country.

Krafton Webber's desires were quite

clear to Rowdy Karl. He was a hot-headed, brutal rannigan, and carrying out cold-blooded murder was almost a pleasure to him.

His horse came down the slope, almost reined back on its haunches. Hoofs hit level ground again, and Rowdy Karl fed steel to the animal's flanks, sending it galloping down the dusty trail.

In the next minute he caught sight of the girl. She was riding the pony slowly. She was obviously unsure of her way out of the broken terrain.

Rowdy Karl thundered up and wheeled his horse in front of her pony. She had to rein in.

"Yuh ain't a-goin' anywhere!" the in-bitten young rannigan snarled.

"What do you mean? Let me pass. Your boss said I had to go free!"

"Webber was jest foolin' yuh!" sneered Rowdy Karl. "Yuh ain't goin' to Monument City. Yuh ain't goin' anywhere."

His hand hovered near the black butt of a six-gun.

She recoiled in horror.

"You can't—you can't stop me! You—"

"Webber don't like folks to know too much about this hideout," sneered Rowdy Karl. "He said I had tuh go an' git yuh afore yuh got away. I'm a-goin' to do thet, but first I got a better idee. Reckon I never got thet kiss we was talkin' about."

His range-hardened arms shot out and gripped her. She was pulled from the saddle. Rowdy Karl attempted to hoist her on to his horse, but she had plenty of youthful strength and she succeeded in resisting. Her feet touched the ground. With a great effort she wrenched free. In a second she was running frantically. She lost her head and forgot about her pony standing near by.

With a coarse laugh Rowdy Karl leaped from his saddle and ran after the girl. To him the chase added zest to the proceedings.

He caught up with the girl as she found herself at bay against a great slab of rock. He reached out and gripped her shoulders again. She fought him, anger and contempt giving her supreme strength.

"Yuh can't git away from me!" rasped Rowdy Karl. He seemed to imagine the triumph of brutality over helplessness was a great thing.

There was a crunching movement in the surrounding brush. A man emerged swiftly. Rowdy Karl wheeled in sharp reaction as the man barked: "Lay off, Karl!"

Rowdy got an impression of a tall man whose face was masked by a yellow bandanna tied around the nose and mouth and knotted at the back of the head.

The outlaw rannigan froze for less than a second, and then his hands clawed for guns.

Rowdy Karl knew it was showdown.

Simultaneously the masked man scooped at hardware. Colts roared death. With Rowdy Karl it was desperate, savage gun-slinging. With the masked man it was gun-play of unbelievable swiftness.

Rowdy Karl staggered back under the

terrible impact of two .45 slugs tearing at his body. His claw for guns had been beaten by sheer speed, although he had gone for hardware first. When his guns had exploded, he had already been moving back under the agonising pain of heavy slugs entering his body.

His bullets had winged upwards, missing the masked man by inches—but missing completely.

Rowdy Karl fell to the ground in a slow, crumpling action. As he thudded to the shale, he was dead. He sprawled, guns falling a yard to one side. Blood seeped from his body, pumped on by the last action of his heart.

Jean Marsh stiffened and closed her eyes. For a moment she stood thus, beating back the horror of seeing violent death. Then she was brought back to reality by the gruff voice of the masked man.

"Git on yore pony, Miss. Yuh kin git to Monument, I reckon. Don't worry none about yore father. He'll be all right, I figger."

She opened her brown eyes.

"Who are you?"

"Jest forget thet, will yuh? Git to leather. I got plenty to do."

"You saved my life," she gasped. "He was ready to kill me! I don't know who you are—how you came to be here—"

"I said to forget it, Miss!" snapped the man. "Now git to thet pony afore he strays."

He watched her vault to the saddle. He waved slightly, and she rode on down the trail. In a minute she was lost to his sight among the rocky land with its clumps of scrub, cactus and juniper.

He dragged Rowdy Karl's body into a crevice in the rocks. Swiftly he heaped stones over the body so that the prowling coyote and vulture would not get a carrion meal. He threw Rowdy Karl's guns in the crevice. Then he grabbed at the dead rannigan's horse.

Some minutes later the masked man was mounted on a roan and he was leading the dead outlaw's horse out of the broken land to the comparative plain.

There he stripped the animal of the saddle and hid the gear beneath some rocks. He slapped the horse with a rifle-butt and watched it gallop in fright. The horse would be lost for a few days.

Quickly, he turned his own cayuse and rode pretty fast into the maze of rock-lined paths that led right into the broken terrain.

In the outlaw hideout, Krafton Webber was breathing heavily as he lay back and regarded Doc Marsh. The old doc was wiping his set of instruments and placing them back in a leather case which rolled up.

"The bullet is out and the wound is clean," said Doc Marsh. "Yuh'll have no further trouble. I guess it'll heal rapidly. Maybe it'll be stiff for some days. Avoid movin' yore shoulder until the tissue heals."

"Yuh done fine," muttered Krafton Webber. "Better than any ham-handed cuss."

"I take it I can go on my way now," said Doc Marsh.

He placed his instrument roll in his store suit pocket and stared with dignity at Webber's sardonical face.

"Yuh kin stick around until I git to feelin' a lot better," growled Krafton Webber. "Mebbe another day or two will see me in the saddle."

"Yuh'll be a remarkably hard man if you can ride in another two days," said Doc Marsh.

"I bin wounded afore and rode pretty soon after it!" snapped the other.

"So I notice. Wal, perhaps you can lend me a horse so that I can join my daughter? After all, I have done you a service, sir. You don't need me any more. There is no need for me to stay another day."

But Doc Marsh was wasting his breath.

Krafton Webber jerked his head to Texas Callahan.

"Take this durned idjut to a shack an' lock him in! Thet's enough fer the time bein'."

65

Texas Callahan grinned unpleasantly.

"Shore, boss. Anythin' yuh say. Mebbe it's a good idee to keep this jigger hyar until we git the other old-timer. Mebbe we c'd use a doc. Somebody might git hurt."

"I'll think about it," returned Krafton Webber. "All right, git this cuss to the shack an' lock him up."

"Damn you!" roared Doc Marsh. "I demand to go my way! I want to join my daughter and attend to my business."

"Ef yuh join yore daughter," grinned Krafton Webber, "yuh'll shorten yore life, hombre!"

The sinister meaning of the words struck Doc Marsh like a blow. He was helpless when Texas Callahan prodded him with a Colt.

"You tricked me!" gasped the old fellow. "By Gawd, if you've harmed Jean—"

"Git goin'!" snarled Webber. "I want tuh smoke an' rest!"

Out in the clearing, between the shacks, Texas Callahan met Jed Ryland.

Texas pushed the old doc into a shack made of split logs and rammed the wedging bar in position.

"Thet accounts for him," he chuckled. "Now mebbe the boss will git to thinking about ropin' Andrew Platt good an' proper. Yuh goin' in fer chow, amigo?"

Jed Ryland leaned against the shack and leisurely brought out the makings for a cigarette.

"I've had chow. Shore is good grub hyar. But when does my five hundred dollar investment show a dividend?"

Texas Callahan slapped him on the shoulder.

"When Webber gits the location of thet bonanza, yuh'll be mighty glad yuh came in with us."

Jed Ryland nodded calmly and struck a sulphur match to light his cigarette. Texas Callahan walked away to the chuckhouse. The Irish-Mexican walked with a roll, his thumbs jammed in his belt. Jed watched him depart with a fixed smile.

Some hours later, after the brassy sun began to slant down again from its midday height, Krafton Webber apparently thought out a new plan for getting control over Andrew Platt. He called for Texas Callahan. He walked slowly on to the porch of his shack and slumped to a chair. He used his good right hand to pour a drink. He threw it down his throat.

"Yuh rannigans got to git thet Platt hombre," he said. "Thar ain't no sense in waitin' another few days till I kin ride with yuh. Texas, git five—six men. Ride out to Monument City afore sundown. Mebbe yuh kin nosy around and git thet blamed feller Platt."

"All right, we'll see what we kin do," said Texas Callahan. "I figger we're jest as ready to git started after the gold as anyone. I'll git Rowdy Karl and some others."

"Ain't seen Rowdy fer some time," called a man assembled with the others.

"Where'n hell's thet hombre gone?" snarled Krafton Webber. "Go look fer him an' tell him to come hyar while we're makin' plans."

One of the outfit went striding off to look in the bunkhouse. The man who had called out kept muttering something about not seeing Rowdy Karl in spite of looking all over the camp for him.

"The way I see it yuh jest got to locate thet hombre and pick him up," argued Krafton Webber. "It ain't no use making plans. Look what happened the other night? Jest have another try at gittin' thet feller. Yuh all stand to benefit. Yuh know thet. Once we git him hyar, we kin make him talk. He'll talk sense, too, which is more than he'd do ef yuh just stuck a gun at him in Monument City an' asked him fer the location of the bonanza."

"He'd figger to fool anyone who tried thet," agreed Texas Callahan.

"Shore. Wal, yuh kin ride now. Git Rowdy along with yuh. Thet jigger's bin itching for gun-play for a lawng time. He ain't bin real happy since we held up the Laredo stage and killed the guards! Go git thet old Andrew Platt. We want thet wasteland wanderer up hyar."

Webber's decision meant movement in

the camp. Texas Callahan chose his men. He nodded to Jed Ryland for one, and named three others. One was Pedro, a sallow, grinning Mexican. Another was a man called Chub Negler, a squat, hairy gun-slinger. The third was Pete O'Hara, another fighting ruffian.

Texas went stamping around the camp to look for Rowdy Karl. When he couldn't find him he growled angrily.

"Thet hombre's on the lam to El Centro, I guess. Webber don't like jiggers taking things into their own hands."

Texas went back to Krafton Webber to report his guess.

"He's a doggone hell-bent fool!" snapped the boss. "Wall, yuh'll have to git along without him. If he's in El Centro a-drinkin' his blamed head off, I'll have him flogged."

Some time later the party rode out in single file. Five grinning, joking men armed with guns and rifles cantered horses through the paths among the thousand rocky outcrops.

The riders did not hustle the horses at

the outset. For one thing they had plenty of time as yet. They knew it was not much good for them to ride into Monument City before sundown. They intended to make a slow journey there, and, in all probability, a fast one back.

The men were bound by one grim purpose. They had a real interest in bringing Andrew Platt back to the camp with them.

They reached the points which showed the trail to their experienced eyes and cantered on, two riders abreast.

For no obvious reason, Jed Ryland was behind the other four men. Tall in the saddle, he rode quietly behind the owl-hoots. He kept his eyes on their backs. His blue eyes were cold and narrowed.

The five riders reached flatter land where grass grew in sparse tufts. Miles away, out of the hills and the heat hazes, Monument City lay at the extreme end of the huge valley. As yet, they were on the fringe of the flat country.

All at once a horse trotted out of a

clump of scrub oak. Riderless, saddleless, the animal swung to the party of five.

Texas Callahan was the first to draw rein.

"Hell, ain't thet Rowdy Karl's hoss?"

"That's right, amigo," agreed Pedro. "But where is the saddle?"

Texas Callahan halted his horse grimly.

"Say, what goes on? This is Rowdy Karl's hoss, all right. What the heck's happened to him? Thet's rannigan's missing, ain't he? Now his hoss turns up wi' no saddle!"

4

NO answers were forthcoming from the dumb animal, and so Texas Callahan slapped the horse away. He was puzzled and suspicious. He stared around the arid land with his black eyes clouded with anger. He was already thinking the worst. But he could not understand exactly what had happened. He did know, however, that Rowdy Karl had taken saddle after the freed girl.

"Say, didn't Rowdy git after thet gal? Reckon he took this hoss, too. Wal, now what the heck happened? Thet gal didn't pack a gun—an' she couldn't trick Rowdy wi' a gun even if she had one."

"Rowdy had his orders, hadn't he?" queried Jed Ryland.

"Yep. Shore had. Webber gave him the wink to blast thet gal."

"There was some shootin'," grunted

Chub Negler. "I reckon I heerd some shots. More'n one, I figger."

Texas Callahan stared.

"Ef Rowdy was blastin' thet gal, he might use more'n one shot."

"C'd have bin some hombre blastin' Rowdy," growled the hairy gun-slinger.

"Thet's plumb crazy!" snapped Texas. "There ain't bin any cusses up hyar. Nuthin' but rattlers up hyar."

"Wal, it's durned queer!"

"The hell with Rowdy Karl!" snarled Texas. "Thet jigger is either dead or he ain't. We ain't got time to ride back and tell Webber about this an' mebbe it don't matter. Let's git!"

They rode on, a sullen, thoughtful party of tight-lipped men. Only one man seemed unconcerned. A thin smile hovered on Jed Ryland's lips.

They rode down out of the broken lands and entered upon the plain that narrowed—in a comparative sense—into the valley. The riders kept off the trails because they did not want to meet anyone. They rode past herds of beef, and never thought of the value of stolen steers to the railroad crews one hundred miles away in Laredo. Rustling beef was a thing of the past, for the moment. They had bigger ideas on hand. They had visions of unlimited gold.

The horizon reddened and streaked with colours as it prepared to receive the descending sun. The riders jogged on, in no hurry to get to Monument City. Only nightfall favoured them. They were all wanted men, and posters bearing their descriptions, and sometimes pictures, decorated the office wall of the sheriff of Monument City.

They did, in fact, halt beneath a thick clump of cottonwoods, some four miles out of the town. The sky was flaring with red and gold. The dusk was light enough for riders to be recognised.

Motionless in the saddles, close to the tree boles, the five riders waited. One or two rolled cigarettes, smoking them with cupped hands.

Then Jed Ryland said softly, "I got a plan, Texas. Why not one feller ride on ahead and locate Andrew Platt. One man can move around pretty easy. Once the old galoot is found, this rider c'd ride out and join up wi' the main party again. Then we all ride in and make a job of it this time."

"Reckon thet's a fair idee," returned Texas Callahan.

"I'll ride in if yuh like," said Jed Ryland easily. "I kin locate this old hombre. Nobody will ever see me around. Anyway, not many know my pan even if they see me. I'm a stranger."

"Thet suit you jiggers?" drawled Texas Callahan.

"I reckon so," grunted Chub Negler, and the others grunted agreement.

"All right. Give me half an hour," said Jed Ryland. "I notice there's a ruined mission jest before yuh enter town. I'll meet up with yuh lot there. Mebbe I'll ha' found Andrew Platt; or mebbe it's a dead duck."

He jigged his horse forward and cantered at a half lope to the town.

It was sufficiently dark when Jed

Ryland entered the town and passed down the main street for him to pass un-recognised. For a member of an owl-hoot outfit, he acted rather strangely.

He rode straight up to the sheriff's office and hitched his horse to the tie-rail.

Then he walked steadily round to the back of the two-story building of wood and brick. He rapped on the door with an unusual pattern of light blows.

The door opened and Sheriff Ezra Strang stared out into the darkness.

"I've come to give myself up," said Jed Ryland, and he laughed.

"Yuh doggone hellion!" grunted Ezra Strang. "What'n heck are yuh doin' in town now? Come right in afore anyone sees yuh."

Jed Ryland walked coolly into the passage, stared around and then went down to the door that gave access to the office proper. In the other room, Sheriff Strang lived. He was unmarried and could cook as good as any woman or Chinaman.

"What's on yore mind, Jed?" asked

Ezra Strang, staring with grim eyes at the younger man.

"Four of Webber's outfit was waitin' in a clump of cottonwoods outside the town," said Jed Ryland. "I've got to locate Andrew Platt, an' then ride out an' lead the other rannigans in. They figger to pick up Platt to-night, git him to Webber's camp and make him talk."

"Platt could fool 'em!" grunted Ezra Strang.

"I don't think so. Webber intends to take the old-timer along when they ride into the badlands after the gold."

"Yuh told me all this last night," grunted the sheriff.

"Shore did. Webber accepted me when I rode back to his camp next morning. I told him I couldn't find the trail in. They believed thet. As a matter o' fact, it was kinda tough finding the way up thet broken territory. I wasn't foolin' when I told yuh last night it wasn't time yet to take a posse up to the hideout."

"Maybe yuh kin lead us up this time," suggested Ezra Strang.

"I'm goin' to lead four jiggers right into yore hands," said Jed Ryland grimly. "After thet mebbe we kin ride up an' clear the rannigans out o' thet camp. Webber got plugged in the shoulder last night, but Texas Callahan jest got a hole in his hat."

"Yuh should aim straighter!" barked Sheriff Strang.

"When I started thet rumpus outside yore office last night, I did aim straight," retorted Jed. "But the durned hosses spoiled the play. Thet was my fault fer slapping Andrew Platt's bay so darned hard. Anyway, I missed Webber's heart. I had to do somethin'. I didn't figger to let him take thet old-timer up to this camp so thet he could work on him."

"I'm only itching to clean them outlaws out o' this territory," snapped Ezra Strang. He began reaching for his Winchester rifle.

"Maybe we kin do it to-night," retorted Jed Ryland. There was grimness in his blue eyes. With hat pushed back to reveal straw-coloured hair, he looked a splendid specimen of manhood.

"I figger we set yuh up wi' a reputation!" chuckled Ezra Strang. He tightened his ammunition belt. "When we chased after yuh into El Centro, I shore laid it on thick to those no account hellions."

"Yeah, they figger I'm a bank robber. Especially when I had the real money," grinned Jed.

"Yuh ain't had a chance to blast Webber yet?" queried the sheriff.

"I've had one or two chances, Ezra. But we want the whole durned bunch. Maybe I could have blasted Krafton Webber, but thet wouldn't git me out o' the camp alive. I thought about it on the ride down last night, but figgered to wait. Then when I really slung lead at them, the hosses started to tangle the play. I had a chance to throw lead at the four who rode down with me to-night, but shooting four jiggers in the back ain't my line, Ezra. An' to warn them was kinda makin' it tough fer me. Anyway, thet wouldn't account fer Webber. Nope. I reckon we stand a chance o' tightening the loop tonight. I'll bring those four gents in near to Andrew Platt's house. Yuh got time to round up a posse. But for Gawd's sake, don't plant lead in me!"

"We'll watch out for yuh!" said the sheriff with grim satisfaction.

"Fine. Just one more thing. I had to kill Rowdy Karl."

"Huh? How come? Shore will save the job o' hangin' thet varmint."

"Webber has a doc—Doc Marsh—held in his camp. Webber's rannigans rode out and lifted this old doc out o' his caravan. The old-timer has a daughter. Webber let her go and then sent Rowdy Karl after her. I jest saw the play and—wal—I went after Karl. I beat him to the draw."

Sheriff Ezra Strang grabbed his Stetson, rammed it firmly on his head and tightened the loop.

"Shore yuh beat him on the draw, podner. Yuh're a Texas Ranger, ain't yuh? Yuh're the hombre I got from San Antonio. Yuh're the Ranger Captain

Bellamy sent me to help clear Webber out o' this territory. Nobody knows yuh because this place is a long way from San Antonio."

And the sheriff shouldered forward. He was ready to get his horse from the livery at the back of his office.

Jed Ryland fumbled in a secret pocket of his belt. He brought out a badge. It was a gleaming silver star set in a silver circle—the feared and honoured badge of the Texas Rangers. Jed rubbed it slightly and then put it back in the hidden pouch. No one would find it there—unless he was dead!

"All right," he muttered. "Let's git. Yuh've got time to lay yore posse-men around Platt's house, sheriff. I'll lead those jiggers right in. Don't plug me. I can't digest lead."

And with that grim humour, the two men slipped out into the night. Jed walked quickly to his horse and leaped to the leather. He swung the animal's head and galloped down the dark street.

The plan was laid.

The way Jed Ryland saw it the four owl-hoots would be led into a trap. After that, if they were dead or captured, a posse could be taken up to Krafton Webber's hideout in the broken country. Jed considered he knew the way into the camp now. There would be no fumbling. He could show some of the posse-men the other exit from the camp and so trap the renegades completely. Last night, after the rumpus during which Webber was shot, he had not been sure of the other exit from the camp. And he had been a bit uncertain of finding the right trail in the maze which led to the outlaw hideout. All that had induced him to ride up in the morning and rejoin the outlaw band.

He had wondered whether Krafton Webber had any suspicions, but apparently the fact that he had real stolen money and that Sheriff Strang had chased him were good factors in his favour.

Only Rowdy Karl had taken an instinctive distrust to him. And now Rowdy Karl was dead. The bull-headed rannigan had had a bullet with his name on it for a long time!

As Jed Ryland approached the ruined Spanish mission just outside the town, he blanked out all such reflections and switched his mind to immediate things.

He reined his horse from a full lope to a walk. He moved round the wall of the old place, and by a clump of old cotton-woods, almost as old as the ruins, he found a group of horsemen.

There were sudden, muttered, inquiring greetings. Jed Ryland answered them. Then:

"Thet old galoot is dozing in his chair. He's jest sittin' at home. I reckon I could ha' nearly got him out hyar myself."

"Wal, it's a cinch five o' us kin handle him," chuckled Texas Callahan. "Let's git in thar!"

With a tattoo of hoofs, the horses were swung on to the trail and headed for town.

Jed Ryland rode in the centre of the bunch. But he figured to creep away when the actual approach on Andrew Platt's house was made. The rannigans would have to walk up, he reasoned. Too much noise and they would defeat themselves.

As they rode into town, Chub Negler and Texas Callahan presented their backs to Jed more than once. He had the chance to draw a gun and shoot them dead. But the other two would certainly react swiftly. They would blast him before he could turn a gun on them.

But even with ruffians like these, Jed Ryland could not bring himself to shooting a man in the back. It was not in his strict code. He always figured to give the other man warning. He had no mercy —he would shoot to kill, and he banked on his skill to save his life. But treacherous shooting of another man in the back was not for him.

And if he was reckless enough to hand out a warning, he would face four guns —more because Texas and Chub Negler were instinctive two-gun men.

It all added up to the fact that it was better to lead the outlaws to capture by the appointed sheriff of Monument City.

If the rannigans preferred death to capture, that was their party! They were getting a chance, which was more than they had given many of their victims.

The five men rode in between the false-fronted buildings of the main street, passing a few saloons and one dance-hall. The outlaws turned grim, wary eyes to right and left, ready to deal with any recognition. But fortunately for them, there was little unusual in a group of riders moving into Monument City. Men rode in from the outlying spreads to drink and gamble, and their appearance was like most westerners.

Presently they slowed the horses near to Andrew Platt's neat little home. It was quiet in the street, with only an occasional man lurching from one saloon to another. The owl-hoots dropped boots to the ground. They threw reins over nearby tie-rails. Quietly, they moved to enter Andrew Platt's house by various routes.

Jed Ryland wondered just where Ezra Strang had posted his men. There was nothing to be seen. Nothing moved. The nearest light was from a saloon twenty yards away. The night was fairly dark. Later a moon would ride the sky.

Jed Ryland walked to the boardwalk of a store adjacent to Andrew Platt's house. He flattened against the wall. He was still near enough to the other four outlaws to be considered one of their party. He was watching warily for some signal coming from Sheriff Strang.

The unforeseen happened. The door of Andrew Platt's house opened. The old-timer was seen at the door and there was a girl with him. With great gallantry the old man was escorting the girl from his home.

Jed Ryland felt surprise trickle through him.

The girl had red hair. She was Jean Marsh, the girl he had helped get to Monument City.

The darkness was still silent all around the house. Jed was stiff, waiting for some alarm. All at once he hoped no shooting would start while the girl was on the path leading to the road.

Then dark shapes seemed to leap out of the shrubs of Andrew Platt's little garden. Another two ran round the house to the door.

As the shapes leaped to grapple with Andrew Platt, guns exploded. Red flame belched from across the road and from the veranda of a store near by.

Jed knew Ezra Strang's men were starting a pistol party. The shooting was on.

But the first shots got only one man. Jed, grimly poking his gun around the corner of the building, thought the man who stumbled and fell was Pete O'Hara.

The outlaws were now warned. Jed Ryland waited to get a line on one.

He saw Texas Callahan get hold of the girl and swing her to him. With his great strength, he held her as a shield. He backed across the garden plot, gun in right hand. He went down the darkness on the side of the house. His gun roared twice, spitting flame which gave away his position.

Jed Ryland was nearest to the house.

He saw Chub Negler grapple with Andrew Platt just as the old-timer clawed for a gun. Jed aimed, breathing a prayer that he would not hit the old bonanza owner. He squeezed off the shot and simultaneously the two men rolled to the ground together. Jed figured he had missed Chub Negler. The two fought among the desert plants. There was no possibility of picking off Chub Negler.

Jed Ryland moved forward, step by step. A man arose from behind a bush near the picket fence. Jed stared at Pedro's enraged face. Then guns flashed death.

It was Pedro who staggered back to the earth. His gun had exploded, but the slug shot skywards because the man was moving back under the impact of another bullet.

Jed Ryland moved on at a crouch. During the few seconds that had passed dealing with Pedro, Chub Negler had hauled Andrew Platt to his feet. The old-timer was limp, unconscious. As Jed Ryland turned, the other outlaw hauled

Andrew Platt down the darkness along the side of the house.

Jed snapped a shot into the gloom. It was high enough to hit a man and yet miss the trailing body of Andrew Platt.

A gun belched flame back at him and Jed Ryland felt the slug whine uncomfortably close. He ran up to the wall of the house and flattened against it.

Chub Negler and Texas Callahan had disappeared down the dark side of Andrew Platt's house, and they both had hostages. Grimly, Jed felt that things were going badly. It was not possible to shoot into the darkness indiscriminately. He might hit the red-haired girl or Andrew Platt.

But Pedro and Pete O'Hara were dead.

In swift seconds men ran over the road to close around Andrew Platt's house. The posse-men were grimly anxious to finish off the outlaws.

Jed Ryland decided to risk it. He jumped into the dark passage down the side of the house. He moved along the wall, flatter than a shadow. Peering ahead grimly, he expected a gun to roar at him any moment.

He guessed Texas Callahan and Chub Negler had made for the livery at the rear of the house. That was it. They expected to get horses. For they knew they could not return to their own mounts hitched to the tie-rail in the main street.

Jed Ryland reached the end of the house wall. He stopped for a moment; then heard the sound of horses' hoofs. The animals were being led out hurriedly, he knew, judging by the sounds.

A voice shouted thickly:

"Yuh kin stay back, Ryland, yuh durned snake. I got a gal an' Chub has Platt! Shoot an' yuh'll durned plug one o' 'em! I seen yuh, Ryland! I'll git yuh, snake!"

For answer Jed threw a slug into the air ahead of him. Then he had to flatten as Colts roared back angrily.

When the echoes died away, he was conscious of hoof-beats thudding hard-baked earth. Texas Callahan and Chub Negler were off with their hostages!

Simultaneously men crowded up behind Jed Ryland. First among them was Ezra Strang. Swiftly he pinned a deputy badge to Jed's shirt. It was the work of a second. It was also the work of a second for the sheriff to mumble through the scant words that made Jed Ryland a deputy sheriff. Then the men dug heels to earth as they raced for horses.

Jed got his roan. The horse reared at first as Jed vaulted to the saddle. The shooting had spooked the other horses, but they remained tied to the rail. Jed dug rowels at his roan. Hoofs pounded the hard earth as rider and animal sped off. Another second and the posse-men were running to round up their horses. But they had not reckoned on pursuit, and time was wasted. Jed Ryland found himself well in the lead. In fact, as he thundered out of town, the posse were a long way behind him.

He thought the shooting parley had gone rather badly even if two of the outlaws were dead. But he had not reckoned on Andrew Platt appearing at his door with the girl.

Jed Ryland wondered what the girl was doing visiting the old-timer. She could not know him, for she had been travelling with her father. It was a rather mysterious feature but it did not alter the fact that Platt and she had walked into an ambush.

So far as he could see the pretence of being a wanted man was finished. Texas Callahan had seen him—probably shooting at Pedro. Texas would guess who had set the ambush.

Jed Ryland was ahead of the posse. He used his rowels on the roan, getting the utmost out of the gallant animal.

He figured that Texas Callahan and Chub Negler were handicapped with double loads. It was only a matter of time before he caught up with their overloaded horses.

Jed knew the trail out of Monument City now. He knew the way the two outlaws would head.

The ruined mission was passed. He urged his horse on, risking the animal plunging a hoof into a jack-rabbit hole. Night riding at full lope was always risky.

The town, with its winking yellow lights, was left behind and he was thundering over the range where the aroma of sage floated up with hoof dust. Somewhere ahead were the two desperate, wanted men. They had two passengers, one of whom was very valuable to them.

For some strange reason, Jed Ryland felt pretty anxious about the red-haired girl. He admired her pluck. She had stood up to Rowdy Karl mighty fine.

Head down to lessen wind resistance, he crouched along the roan's neck. Staring ahead, he thought he saw a dark bobbing shape.

He thrust a hand to his gun, cocked it. He pointed it ahead, clear of the roan's bobbing mane.

And then, all at once, he had to swerve the horse violently to avoid a person standing as if transfixed in the animal's path.

Jed Ryland drew the roan up, turned

back and cantered close to the pale face staring out of the darkness.

"Goshdarn—you!" he ejaculated.

It was Jean Marsh.

He got down from his horse and walked to her.

She was clad in checked shirt and blue jeans. She wore a fawn hat over her red hair. She looked absurdly boyish in the dim night light.

"So yuh escaped!" he laughed. "How'd yuh do it?"

He was very near to her. She stared into his face and looked startled. Her next reaction was unexpected.

She flung herself at him. Her fists beat at him. He whipped a hand to grab her wrists. She slipped one hand away and scooped at his Colt butt.

The next second he was staring at the gun rammed into his middle!

"You doggone skunk!" she panted. "You're one o' them! I know you! Doggone dirty outlaws!"

"Hey. Wait a minute!" Jed Ryland almost found himself yelping. There was a streak of amusement in the core of grim threat. "I'm not an outlaw."

"I saw you in the camp! You were the one who stopped that terrible feller from kissing me. Mebbe you had reasons of yore own!"

He pointed to the deputy badge.

"The name's Jed Ryland, Miss. Shore I was in Webber's camp. Mebbe I kin tell yuh more if yuh give me back my gun."

He knew a trick to knock down a pointed Colt, especially when the one pointing was not too experienced, but he hesitated to start it. First he would talk.

"Mebbe yuh don't remember the jigger who shot Rowdy Karl when he came after yuh?"

Uncertainty began to chase over her face. She was certainly surprised.

"How'd you know—?"

"Why, that hombre was me, Miss Jean. Now hand over my gun?"

In her uncertainty, she had allowed it to drop a little. He flashed out brown hands and in a second, as if by magic, he held the gun again. Another second, and it was dropped into his holster.

"Git up in front o' me," he said grimly. "Yuh'll have to go back to town. Mebbe we catch the posse ridin' out. I shore hope so, because I aim to git after Krafton Webber to-night. Kin yuh tell me what you were doing at Andrew Platt's house?"

"Why, he saw my caravan and asked me to make up some ointment. That's all. I was just talkin' to him. Those doggone skunks have taken him off! They got him just like my father. How is my father—do you know?"

He helped her up in front of his saddle and started back in the direction of the town. He resented the delay and yet the nearness of this girl had a strange fascination. A hard man, he had spent most of his time riding in the course of duty and women had had little part in his life.

"I guess yore dad is all right for the moment," he replied. "But we got to smash Webber afore he takes an ugly mood. He shore will when he learns about to-night."

"I still don't understand who you are," she pointed out.

"Wal, Miss Jean, yuh kin see I'm a sheriff's deputy at the moment. I guess the play with Webber is all washed up. I'm a Texas Ranger, Miss Jean, and I've got a mission to bust up Krafton Webber's outfit. They've spent long enough raisin' trouble in this territory. It's a lawng story, but I was accepted by Webber as a member of his outfit. But thet's all bust up. Texas Callahan knows the truth now."

And then, before she could ask any more questions, they rode into the posse thundering in a wide sweep over the range. Seeing Jed Ryland with the girl, there was a moment of confusion until Ezra Strang bawled out words.

The posse halted around Jed Ryland. Horses were blowing and pawing the earth.

"Yuh'll have to ride back with one o' the posse-men," said Jed to the girl. "We're a-goin' up to Webber's hideout. I don't like this delay, either."

"I'm not going back to town!" flashed the girl. "I have every right to go after my own father if I want to. I'm coming with you, Deputy Ryland!"

There was a guffaw among the assembled men.

"Yuh can't ride up thar!" snapped Jed. "Besides yuh ain't got a hoss."

"I'll ride with you," retorted the girl.

"That'll plumb tucker my hoss out before the night's finished."

There was a call from one of the possemen.

"A hoss has bin ridin' along with me since we lighted out o' town. I figger it's one of the outlaw's critters. Jest galloped out with us and kept alongside."

"Seems the cards play yore way," said Jed curtly. "But this ain't woman's work."

"What is woman's work?" she flashed.

He changed the subject.

"Yuh didn't tell me how yuh got away from Texas?"

"He just set me down. He didn't have

time to shoot me, I guess. The double load was slowing his hoss."

"You were lucky," declared Jed Ryland. "All right, let's git after 'em! Ezra, these fellers know who I am?"

"Shore do!"

"Thet's fine. But those durned hombres have a head-start. Git to thet stray hoss, Miss Jean, and stick close."

"I'll stick to you," she said.

In a minute the posse thundered on again. Some ten riders fed steel to mounts. In a dust-raising bunch, the horsemen went on. For an hour they journeyed across the dark valley and then turned in a body and entered the first winding trail through the hills. Jed Ryland, as the only man who knew the secret routes to the hideout, was head of the posse. Sticking closer to him than a brother was Sheriff Ezra Strang. And right beside him, Jean Marsh contrived to keep her horse.

The horses slowed to walking pace many times in the next hour. Only infrequently could the posse jog the animals to a canter. There were only a few patches of clear ground between the hundreds of rocky outcrops. At no time did the posse sight the fleeing outlaws.

Grimly and silently, the men jogged the horses on through the occasional clumps of scrub timber and brush. Once a coyote howled from a hilltop. The moon was creeping into sight between thin, idle clouds. They climbed into the hilly broken country where gaunt Joshua trees stood like skeletons.

Then after another hour of climbing slithering shale slopes or wending through twisting, rocky gullies, Jed Ryland halted his horse before the jagged rocky pile-up which hid Krafton Webber's camp. Over the rocks was a canopy of trees, sycamore and juniper. They grew from holes between the rocks. They certainly hid the camp.

"There are only two ways into this camp with a hoss," grunted Jed Ryland. "And I figger thet crafty hombre will have a man posted to each path. It ain't easy to git in there. Reckon there's about a thousand holes where a jigger could lie waitin' with rifle and gun. Nope, we'll have to climb through those clefts and ledges—on hands and knees."

"Wal, we never got this close to them hombres before," grunted Ezra Strang. "All right. We kin hitch the hosses up to some trees an' leave a feller on guard. The rest will have to find a way through thet pile-up. Shore is a regular mix-up of rock."

"Volcanic, I guess," said Jed.

The men gathered around, and he gave a swift description of the layout ahead. He described how the tumbled rocks and outcrops circled the clearing, and how the trees helped to hide the paths. He stressed that Webber would certainly have sharp-shooters posted to watch the twisting paths.

Then they went forward, each man creeping and climbing the jumble of volcanic rock. Jed Ryland took the girl's arm.

"I reckon I got to look after yuh," he said grimly.

"I was brought up pretty rough an' ready," she answered. "I can take care of myself."

"Hunting these men is not work for a woman!" he snapped.

"There you go again! Well, I'm determined to help get my father out of there."

There was nothing to do but take her along. Jed Ryland helped her once or twice, only to discover she could climb and slither through jagged cracks in the pile-up as well as he! After moving forward, almost parallel with the twisting path on the right, he handed her a gun.

"Yuh might need this!" he breathed.

He was carrying a rifle. He jumped to a ledge, pulling himself up and sliding along flat. Then followed a moment's pause while he peered grimly into the gloom ahead. The chunks of volcanic boulders made deep patches of velvet darkness. Above them, the light was not as deep. The moon was casting a faint radiance over the scene.

All at once he heard a gun explode near by. The slug did not come his way.

Apparently the shot was fired at one of the posse. Jed saw the flame and knew from the position it was one of the outlaws. He whipped his rifle level and sent a steel-jacketed bullet right to the spot where the gun had flashed.

The fight was on!

5

GUNS began to roar from all directions and some of them were rifles. In the dark it was difficult to assess just who was friend and who was foe. But the outlaws gradually crept back to certain positions which made it obvious they were defending. Jed Ryland thought he had got his first man because he had heard a yell of rage.

The laborious climbing through cholla-filled cracks and clefts went on. Gun-flashes stabbed the night just ahead. Jed Ryland piled a few rifle-shots into the positions which were undoubtedly occupied by the owl-hoots. As his shots died away, he flattened to the rock. He pushed Jean Marsh down beside him. As he expected, answering fire whined and pinged all around them.

Jed Ryland lay, staring at the girl's pale face close to his.

"This ain't no place . . ." he began.

". . . for a woman!" she finished.

"Wal, it ain't!" he snapped.

He poked the Winchester out and waited grimly for some target to present itself.

As he waited, he realised there was a curious silence ahead. Behind him and on his right and left, he knew the posse-men were still hugging the rocks. But ahead there was this silence and the lack of gunfire.

Jed Ryland triggered a shot ahead. The echoes died away. There was no return fire. No prompt gun-flash came back. He looked into Jean's eyes.

"I figger they're gittin' out. Unless they're hidin' in the shacks."

He began to slither forward again. Jean followed. Seeing their movement, a few of the posse-men crept on again, some jumping from cover to cover, others thrusting up cactus-filled crevices. No shots stabbed through the night to stop them. Seeing this, the posse-men went forward with increasing speed. Ezra

Strang's voice could be heard bawling instructions and advice.

Jed Ryland reached the edge of the rocky ramparts conscious that Jean was still behind him. He felt some admiration for her in the way she had stuck it.

He stared ahead at the dark outlines of the shacks. He swung his keen blue eyes and stared at the horse corral.

He turned and sat up. He shouted the facts back to the posse-men.

"The hosses are not in the corral! I figger they've got out the other path!"

Dark shapes of men leaped down from the rocks and hugged the grass of the clearing. Then, a second or two later, they ran forward, guns levelled. But no shots hacked out redly from the shacks. The posse ran on at a crouch, came to the first shack. One man knocked the door in. The place was obviously empty.

Taking Jean Marsh by the arm, Jed Ryland raced over the ground to the shack which had served as a jail for her father. He noted the wedging-bar was not in position. The fact struck him grimly, like a cold wave of water. He kept the girl to one side. He thrust the door open and stared into the shack.

What he saw angered him terribly. A black shape huddled on the earth floor. He knew before he turned the man over that Doc Marsh was dead. He had been shot cold-bloodedly, as Krafton Webber had decided.

In that second Jed Ryland blamed himself. It was a bit unreasonable, but he felt he might have been able to get the old fellow out of the camp earlier. He did not know how—there was no real way—but he wished he had attempted to get Doc Marsh away. It had been left too late.

Jed Ryland tried to keep the girl out of the dark shack and its horrible exhibit, but the girl would not be deterred. She knew what had happened.

She did not cry. She just bent over her father's body and seemed to stay still and numb for some time. Jed Ryland had to leave her. There was nothing anyone could do. Words of consolation were futile. And he was not the man to babble like a fool.

He went out to contact Ezra Strang. When he reached the burly sheriff, the posse-men had gone through the entire camp and found the outlaws had flown.

"They've taken Andrew Platt," growled Ezra Strang.

"Thet's to be expected," lipped Jed. "He's the trump card. If they git thet gold o' his, they'll light out o' this territory altogether."

"One way o' gittin' rid o' the varmints!" growled the sheriff.

"They've killed Doc Marsh," said Jed grimly. "I reckon thet's plain murder."

"Nuthin' to those doggone skunks!" muttered the other.

In another minute Jean Marsh had to be led away from her dead father. Her face glowed pale in the thin moonlight, and she seemed to turn to Jed Ryland and Ezra Strang for help.

But the chase was still on. As soon as the camp was seen to be empty, Jed Ryland urged the posse-men to follow him down the path through the rock cleft to the area where the horses were hitched.

"Mebbe we kin catch up with those hellions!" roared Ezra Strang. "I want 'em dead!"

As they ran through the foliage-covered cleft, they found a dead outlaw. They guessed one or two more would be still in the rocky pile-up.

One posse-man volunteered to carry Doc Marsh's body out to the horses.

But when the men burst out of the narrow cleft there was a surprise waiting for them.

The man guarding the hitched horses had been dry-gulched. He was dead, sprawled on the ground. The horses were not tied to the trees any longer. They had obviously been stampeded. It was an old trick to foil pursuit. One of the outlaws had evidently ridden around the fringe of the rocky pile-up to achieve the job.

Ezra Strang's cursing was particularly bitter. He seemed to forget that a number of outlaws were dead. Krafton Webber had apparently escaped with only about five men. Jed Ryland and the posse had put paid to two in Monument City.

The sheriff's men went to search the land for the stampeded horses. Jed Ryland walked down a natural trail between tall rock outcrops, giving a peculiar whistle which his roan would recognise.

Half an hour later the men had the animals rounded up. Some had strayed pretty far; others were just nosing for grass in gullies and draws. Presently all were mounted again, but this fact did not prevent Sheriff Ezra Strang from swearing hard. Only when he remembered that there was a girl present did he stutter into decent speech.

"Wal, anyway, we got them out o' this durned hideout," stated the sheriff. "Mebbe thet's somethin'."

It was a definite factor, but he knew they had to start trailing the outlaw gang.

Jed Ryland led the way around to the other exit. One of the posse-men had died because he had got close to the escaping renegades. They found his body hanging limply on a ledge.

The sight made Ezra Strang downright angry.

"Thet's Jim Turner! Hell, I'll have to tell his widder when we git back! I reckon to clean them durned owl-hoots right out o' life when I sight 'em!"

Picking up the trail in the dark was almost an impossible business even to an expert at trailcraft like Jed Ryland. He progressed a good deal from the exit for the hideout, but came to a halt when the land sloped into shale and rock. Ahead in the darkness were at least four ways the men could have gone. It was impossible to discover the sign in the dim moonlight even when he got down from the horse and stared at the ground. He was looking for tell-tale marks of hoofs, dislodged rocks. But it was a heartbreaking task at night. After some hunting, he had to give up.

"Those hellions are well ahead now!" he snapped. "I might make half a mile in the next half-hour. Thet's no durned good!"

Disgruntled, the posse rode back to the outlaw camp.

There was work for them in destroying the place. Soon fires were burning. Krafton Webber's shack was burned to the ground. Then, before a huge fire, the men rested and waited for the dawn.

The men found some food in one of the shacks which had been left behind in the rush to get out. Before the shack was pulled down to provide a fire, the posse-men made use of the grub. Rough and ready, they had bacon and canned beans heated, and they ate. There was nothing to drink but water from a spring which trickled clear and cool from a red cleft in the rocks. This was where the owl-hoots had obtained water.

Before the preparations for the resumption of the trail began, Jed told the girl clearly that she would have to ride back to Monument City.

"This might be a tough ride. Mebbe we won't catch up with those hombres.

Mebbe we won't git Andrew Platt back. So yuh kin see it ain't goin' to be easy. Yuh've got to see your father taken back to town for burial."

She nodded her head in acceptance. He patted her arm awkwardly.

"I'll be waitin' to hear that you've killed those men!" she said fiercely.

"We'll be back," he said. "Mebbe we will kill 'em, at that. Anyway, I'll be back —jest to see you. Yuh ain't leavin' Monument City?"

"Not until I hear about Krafton Webber," she stated. And maybe not—even—then—"

Ezra and Jed started out with five other men. One man was going back with Jean Marsh, helping her to ride the body of her father back to town for decent burial in the town's cemetery—commonly known as Boothill.

Jed Ryland and the others found the sign again. He got past the awkward stretch of shale and found the canyon the outfit had taken the night before. After that they had just momentary stops to examine and debate further sign. Only the merest hoof-print was needed to speed them on and on. To their eyes, the sign checked everywhere. They read that a band of riders had passed this way only hours before.

"Mebbe they're aimin' for the border!" Ezra Strang suddenly exclaimed.

"Is Andrew Platt's bonanza in Mexico territory?" asked Jed Ryland.

"I dunno. Thet old galoot keeps thet a strict secret between him an' the moon. He don't trust anybody. No one ever follered him to his bonanza. It may be in Mexico for all thet I know!"

"The old jigger ought to have registered the claim!" growled Jed. "If we don't git Webber, the gold will be in the outlaws' hands. Soon as they git the location, they'll fill Platt full of lead."

The day wore on, with the laborious business of reading sign and then riding forward. Sometimes they made a mistake, seeing a deer sign and thinking it was made by a horse hoof. They had to double back and pick up the real trail again. The sun rose and the heat brought out sweat on man and horse.

Soon it was obvious that the trail was leading over the border. They wended through the broken country, passing magnificent buttes towering like grotesque sentinels. They rode the horses down shale slopes and through sandy canyons filled with Joshua trees and silvery cholla cactus. Now and then they disturbed a rattler. All the time they were drawing nearer to the Mexico border.

Sheriff Ezra Strang was grim. He saw his chances of laying hands on Krafton Webber getting dimmer. If the hellion got over the border, he would be outside Monument City jurisdiction. Ezra could not get the man if he got to the border.

The pursuers had a good idea where the trail would end. They were riding nearer to El Grande, a border town of lawless ruffians. If El Centro, in Texas territory, was a lawless dump, El Grande could top it. It was a bit bigger, but law was completely absent. So far as Ezra Strang knew, there was a Spanish-speaking sheriff—one Jose Petrillio—but he was as crooked as the rest of the inhabitants.

As they expected, the trail sign led right to El Grande. The junkheap of a town sat on the fringe of a desert. There was some browning grass in the vicinity of the town and a few cottonwoods. The streets were thick with alkali dust. As they rode in, half-naked children played in the dust with chickens and dogs. The place looked somnolent under the midday sun. But the outlaws' trail had led here. Maybe they were holed up in the shanty town.

"Yuh know Andrew Platt might not talk right away about the bonanza even if Webber threatened to beat him up," remarked Jed Ryland.

Sheriff Ezra Strang chuckled grimly.

"Ef I know Andrew Platt rightly, thet gink won't talk fer nobody. He's a hard old cuss. I figger he'd sooner die than give thet bonanza to Webber."

Jed wiped sweat from his face. White dust marked his mouth and cheeks.

"Thet's one thing Webber will have to be mighty careful about. If he kills Andrew Platt, he'll be throwing all his chances away."

"Wal, they haven't had time to work on the old desert tramp yet," declared Ezra Strang.

The trouble was they did not know if the outlaws had entered El Grande and then ridden out. The owl-hoots had enjoyed a good start.

As the posse rode in, Ezra Strang warned them:

"Lissen, men, we ain't got no authority hyar. This durned dump is Mexico. But thet don't mean we can't look around. Ef Webber or any o' his gents should kinda try to draw hardware on yuh, I reckon yuh know what to do."

There was a chuckle all round.

They rode right through the main stem of false-fronted buildings, watched by indolent vaqueros. There was no lead, and so they wheeled the horses and rode slowly back. They intended to go into the shade of the biggest saloon, Santa Alicia.

Jed Ryland sighted a man all at once. The hombre had been watching them from a saloon boardwalk. The man tried to dart back through the bat-wing doors.

Jed smiled thinly.

"I figger Webber and his cohorts are still in this town," said he to Ezra. "I've jest seen one o' them owl-hoots."

The sheriff bristled.

"Whar? Dogblastit! Anyways I can't go git him with a gun. This ain't my bailiwick."

"Take it easy," said Jed. "We want to find Andrew Platt. Mebbe we ain't got much authority over here, but we shore ain't goin' back on thet account. Mebbe we kin git the old-timer back to safety. Thet's the main task."

The posse dismounted, hitched horses to the tie-rail outside the Santa Alicia.

They went in, followed by many curious glances. It was cooler inside the saloon or cantina as they were known over the border. The glare of sunlight was absent, too. The men rasped boots over the boards and reached the bar counter.

Most of them had a genuine need for a drink. They got the shots of rye placed before them. They stared around the saloon, at the small knot of gamblers.

There was a staircase at one end of the big wide room and it led to a balcony. There were rooms above, in the first story of the building.

Jed Ryland was staring up at the balcony when he thought he sensed movement. He did not actually see anyone, but he was sure a man had moved down the passage at the top of the balcony.

"Ever git many folks stayin' hyar?" he rapped at the bartender.

The man was not Mexican. He growled back reluctantly: "Shore, we always got some hombres stayin'. All sorts o' fellers pass through this dump."

"I bet they do," grunted Jed Ryland.

He left the counter and walked to the stairs. The bartender watched him. The posse-men leaned against the pine counter and waited. Jed Ryland walked slowly up the stairs.

"Yuh want a room?" snapped the bartender.

Jed turned his head.

"Nope."

"Wal, hombre, it's kinda private up there. Only fer jiggers who want a room."

But Jed Ryland took little notice. He was following a hunch. He had seen some movement. He had also noticed one of Webber's men still in the town. He thought Krafton Webber must be biding his time in El Grande. The man had to make Andrew Platt talk—without killing him! And if Webber was staying in El Grande, he might easily hole up in the biggest saloon. And that place was the Santa Alicia.

Jed got to the top of the stairs. He looked down a passage in which were a few mahogany doors. A faded carpet ran down the passage. The whole place had a musty odour.

The bartender came running up the stairs to him. The man had an angry look on his swarthy features.

"Yuh kin quit walkin' all over the blamed place as if yuh owned it!"

"Yuh kin see who we are," said Jed. "Mebbe yuh know Sheriff Strang of Monument City?"

"Shore I knows him. What the heck do he want hyar? This ain't Texas. Yuh guys got no right to come bustin' in all over this saloon."

"You the owner?"

"Nope. Feller the name of Jose Petrillio owns this saloon."

"The sheriff?"

"Yeah. He's sheriff too!" sneered the bartender. "What of it?"

"Is he in town right now?"

"Mebbe he is an' mebbe he ain't."

"Does he live hyar?"

"Sometimes," grinned the man.

"All right. Go git him."

The man looked defiant. Jed reached out a brown hand and swiftly grabbed the man by his shirt. He brought his other fist up close to the man's discoloured teeth.

"I said go git him! Yuh wouldn't like me to knock those teeth out, would yuh?"

"Aw, damn yuh! I'll go git Jose Petrillio. He'll be takin' a siesta in his room. He won't like me disturbin' him!"

Jed watched the man go down the passage. He knocked on a door and then walked in. He closed the door after him.

Jed Ryland figured he would walk back downstairs to the others. Jose Petrillio could come down and see them. The man was allegedly sheriff of the town. He had to be told that some wanted men had ridden in and were staying in the town.

Jed Ryland did not expect much help from the Mexican sheriff. Judging by Ezra Strang's accounts, the man was as crooked as the ruffians he was supposed to round up!

Some ten minutes later, Jose Petrillio walked down the staircase, his heavy face wreathed in smiles. He was wearing a checked store suit and a gun-belt carrying twin Colts. He had a sheriff's star pinned on the lapel of his coat. He was perspiring freely, but that was his nature and not because he was afraid of anything.

He broke into voluble English.

"What can I do for you, amigos? A drink on the house? Sure, you have ridden far! A drink on Jose Petrillio. What brings you over to this country, amigos? You look for bad men, huh?"

"Yuh good at guessin'," said Ezra Strang. "We've bin trailing a jigger called Krafton Webber and his cohorts. Them fellers are sure bad medicine. They've kidnapped an old feller name o' Andrew Platt. I figger these galoots are in this town, sheriff. I guess you ought to be warned. If yuh kin chase 'em over the border, we'll be waiting for them."

Jose Petrillio fingered his glass.

"These men, I have not seen them. You bet if I see them making trouble, I chase them back to you. How's that?"

"Fine," said Jed Ryland heavily. "Mebbe yuh could start lookin' for Andrew Platt? He's a Texan citizen, an' we don't like him out o' his own territory. Maybe yuh could git a posse and search this burg for this old-timer?"

The sheriff of El Grande smiled greasily.

"Maybe I could, my friends. But at the moment it is too hot. I could not find a posse—you know how it is in Mexico! Now why does this Krafton Webber kidnap an old man? You tell me that, please! I do not understand."

Jed exchanged a significant glance with Ezra Strang.

"This old jigger is kinda rich," snapped Jed. "That's all. If yuh want a posse, we would deputise for yuh. An' we got no objection to startin' a search o' this place right now. Thet all right?"

Jose Petrillio spread his hands.

"I think it would be unwise. In this town we have some hombres of very bad temper, my friends. They would not like to see Texan law men searching El Grande. It is not law, you understand. No. I will tell you what I will do. To-night, when it is cooler, I will get my posse and we shall look for this Andrew Platt."

Jed Ryland drew in a deep breath.

"Shore. Anythin' yuh figger. Let's git out o' hyar, Ezra."

The sheriff and the posse-men turned and stamped out. They left behind a smiling, thoughtful Jose Petrillio.

On the boardwalk, Jed Ryland snapped words at the others.

"Thet old catamount knows durned well thet Webber would be out o' here by sundown. Him and his durned posse! Why thet devil is hidin' Webber, I bet."

"What makes yuh think thet?" asked Ezra Strang.

"Jest a hunch. And I'm sorry to say we kinda made things worse by tellin' Jose Petrillio thet Andrew Platt is rich. Webber wouldn't give thet away. Now Jose Petrillio will be durned curious."

"Yeah? Wal, I guess we'll jest have to hang around."

The seven men went into a cantina on the opposite side of the road, and they settled down at tables near the two windows. They ordered rye and got it. Most of the Mexicans were drinking wine. Some white rannigans in the saloon watched the posse-men curiously and few had any friendliness. Two frowsy senoritas, with off-shoulder blouses, sneered and decided the strangers represented no potential profit.

"Thet durned Jose Petrillio is as crooked as Webber," snapped Ezra Strang in an undertone to Jed. "Yuh're right. This might mix the play. If Jose gits an idee thet there's unlimited gold in Andrew Platt, somethin' might start. Jose kin git hands on some gun-happy hombres in this hole."

"I'm wondering what's happening to Andrew Platt," commented Jed grimly. "Where have they got him? I don't like this waitin'."

"No more'n I do!" returned the sheriff of Monument City.

Looking out of the window, Jed Ryland got an idea for some action.

"See thet Chink eat-house next door to the Santa Alicia," he breathed. "Git the men over there, Ezra. We all go over. I guess there's a back way out o' thet place."

"Are yuh goin' to eat steak? What

d'yuh want with a back way out o' the place?" demanded Ezra Strang.

"I'll leave you lot eating steak," snapped Jed. "I figger there's room for action by one. I'm goin' inside the Santa Alicia. I want a look around those upstairs rooms. One man can do thet best."

Quiet instructions were given to the five posse-men. A minute later the Texans trooped out and across the road.

The Chink restaurant was like most of its kind. A number of bare wood tables and chairs stood in rows. A few customers were inside, downing good grub. From the back of the place, a Chinaman walked to and fro, serving.

"Git your chow," said Jed Ryland. "When thet Chink comes for yore order, I'll nip around the back. I guess China Joe does his own cookin'."

Apart from anything else, the posse-men were ready and willing to tuck into the steaks and coffee the Chinese cook provided. Like all his race, he dished up good cheap food.

Jed Ryland took his opportunity when the Chinaman was talking to Ezra Strang.

He slipped to the back of the shanty. He went through the kitchen, noted the cleanliness and smiled a little. He saw a door and he unbolted it. He slipped out to the rear of the place. He was standing in a narrow alley looking up at the back windows of the Santa Alicia.

He walked steadily across the dusty ground. He looked up at the back of the building. There was a veranda running around the upstair windows, and the supporting posts were right beside him.

Swiftly, Jed Ryland reached up and gripped the ornamental woodwork. Another second and he hauled himself to the first part of the veranda. A few more seconds of climbing, and he was drawing long legs over the rail. He darted to the wall, a blank space between two windows. He waited in case his climb had been noticed.

Had there been any movement from the windows, he had Colts to back up his play. But nothing stirred. He relaxed and crept silently to the nearest window.

He stared in. The room beyond was empty. He slipped past the pane of glass and approached the other window.

He looked into the room cautiously because he did not want to invite a burst of fire from a gun.

He was hardly surprised when he saw a man sitting on a cane chair. That the man was bound to the chair hands and feet and that a gag decorated his mouth, was nothing of surprise either, for the white-haired fellow was Andrew Platt!

The room was otherwise empty, except for a bed and a dressing-table.

Jed Ryland tried the window. It was closed but the catch had not been pushed into place. Apparently Krafton Webber had not thought it necessary seeing that his prisoner was bound.

Jed Ryland slipped the window up and eased his big body inside the room. When he got in, he turned and shut the window again. Left open, it might attract attention of those who knew it should be shut.

Andrew Platt turned beady eyes on Jed Ryland. The old-timer was surprised.

Then Jed saw hatred blaze from the old desert tramp's eyes.

Jed Ryland had an idea what was wrong. As he came up to Andrew Platt and got busy on the ropes with a knife, he whispered:

"Take it easy, feller. I'm Jed Ryland, a Texas Ranger and a friend o' Ezra Strang. I know yuh saw me last wi' Krafton Webber and Texas Callahan when those jiggers got yuh out o' yore house. But thet was part o' a trick to trap those outlaws. I'm not workin' with them. Don't start bawling when I take this gag out o' yore mouth!"

Jed Ryland soon had the gag whipped from the old-timer's white-haired head. Andrew Platt gasped a bit and worked his jaws and spat. Jed hacked at the ropes with his knife. They slipped off in no time. Soon Andrew Platt was free.

But there was a snag.

The old man could not stand. He had been tied up some time and the circulation in his legs had gone numb. When he attempted to stand, he nearly fell over. Jed Ryland had to support him.

"Goldarn it, gimme a gun an' I'll shoot my way out o' this blasted place!" gasped Andrew Platt.

"Ain't a bad idee!" drawled Jed.

"Say, yuh're a Texas Ranger! I don't git it. You helped Webber take me out o' my own durned home thet night!"

"I also slapped yore hoss and spooked the others into stampede," retorted Jed Ryland.

"Goshdarn it! So it was you? I nearly fell offen thet durned hoss. Now ef it had bin a mule, yuh couldn't ha' stampeded a mule. I allus used a mule when I was travelling the desert—though sometimes a burro."

"Wal, never mind about the nags yuh used to ride in the past, old-timer. We've got to get out o' here."

Andrew Platt began rubbing and slapping his legs. He wore tight brown pants tucked into boots. An old, flapping vest over a checked shirt practically completed his outfit. He certainly did not look like a gold-mine owner.

"Webber been workin' on yuh yet, old-timer?" asked Jed.

For answer Andrew Platt rolled up his sleeves. Jed saw angry red wounds which had been made but recently. Blood was not yet dry on the cuts.

"Done thet wi' a knife!" cackled the old-timer. "Figgered to frighten me, I guess! But I don't scare easy. Thet hombre tried to make me talk by drawing a sharp knife over my arms. But I knew he would not cut deep. Yes, sir, they can't fool me. He wouldn't cut deep an' risk me dyin' on him. He was jest as scared o' me dying as I was—mebbe! Then they left me—him an' thet Irish-Mex wi' him! Said as how they'd be back an' I'd talk about the bonanza before night."

"You'll be out o' here," snapped Jed.

He turned to the door. Even as he stepped forward the handle turned.

133

Someone outside was coming in!
Jed Ryland scooped guns into two fists
and waited!

6

THE few seconds that passed seemed to lengthen, and then the door swung in and a man strode forward.

His steps were cut short peremptorily as Jed Ryland rasped: "Hold it, Texas!"

Black, glinting eyes stared down at the two guns pointing straight at him. Texas Callahan froze. His hand was still on the door.

He knew to go for a gun would invite a swift death. It would roar at him in a second, before he could tug a gun clear of leather.

Being a wise man he just stayed motionless. But he found time to talk.

"Howdy, Ryland. Yuh shore move around. Who yuh foolin' this time?"

"At the moment I'm foolin' you," snapped Jed. "Now cut the talk an' turn around."

Very carefully Texas Callahan turned, showing his back to Jed. A slight fear seemed to get into him.

"Yuh ain't gonna shoot me in the back, Ryland? Yuh can't do an ornery thing like—"

"Shut up!" snarled the Texas Ranger.

He reached out and plucked the other's two guns from the holsters. He handed them to Andrew Platt.

"Now git movin', Texas. Go right down this passage an' down the stairs. We're goin' places. If any hombre figgers to stop us, it'll be too bad for yuh!"

In another minute they reached the landing. Then they traversed the corridor with the mahogany doors. There was no interruption. Jed Ryland ushered Texas Callahan along with the guns in his back. Behind them came Andrew Platt, the old fellow's beady eyes gleaming with triumph and his two guns—Texas Callahan's—moving in menacing circles.

The party reached the staircase and began to move down. Before they had gone a few steps, they attracted attention.

A few border ruffians at the bar looked up. Talk ceased abruptly. Some Mexicans sidled away to corners. The bartender's face twisted unpleasantly. He was a white whose brushes with the law in the past had given him a hatred of all lawmen.

"Don't start anythin', amigos," called Jed Ryland. "If yuh do, this hombre will have a bad time."

In utter silence from immobile men, Jed forced his captive towards the batwing doors. As he went to the door he had to partly turn his back to the bar counter.

With a snarl the bartender snatched at a gun lying in a place that was handy for the gun-play that often happened in the saloon.

He evidently thought he could kill Jed Ryland. He figured that the other was occupied with getting Texas Callahan out of the cantina.

The bartender got the gun above the counter in a swift snatch, but that was all. The Colt never exploded.

Jed Ryland's left gun whipped up at

the first sense of movement. Jed had had his back partly to the man but his instincts for gun-play were fully alert.

The left-hand Colt roared death. The slug dug into the bartender's head. He reeled back with an expression of foolishness which rapidly turned to a grimace as death overtook him. The man slid down under his bar.

Seconds before he began to slide, Jed Ryland jabbed at Texas Callahan in a way that meant he wanted quicker movement. Before the echoes of thc gun-shot died away, Jed had forced the other out on to the boardwalk. Andrew Platt clung grimly to the big blond young rannigan.

Men poured out of the Chink eating-house. Ezra Strang was first, with guns in his hands. Seeing Andrew Platt alive and unharmed, he gave a whoop of delight. Ezra gripped the old-timer's arm and hustled him along to the hitched horses.

The posse-men just reached the animals when guns began to roar from upstair windows of the Santa Alicia.

Men jumped to horses. Ezra Strang saw

to it personally that Andrew Platt was mounted on his own saddle.

Jed Ryland made Texas Callahan get up in front of him on the roan. Guns flung lead dangerously close. It was the work of a few seconds, however, for the posse to get mounted, and then, all at once, in a welter of confused shooting, they were riding furiously down the dusty main stem of El Grande.

Ezra Strang had Andrew Platt riding double with him. Jed Ryland thought he would be content to have captured Texas Callahan. Krafton Webber would get rounded up some other time. In seconds the horses were pounding out of El Grande.

The riders were clear of the town in a fast thunder of hoofs, but they were not clear of danger.

Behind them a cloud of dust proved that there was pursuit. Apparently Krafton Webber had sent his remaining rannigans after them. Looking back, Jed could not know if Webber himself was riding. So far the pursuing riders were just a bundle of bobbing horses on the glare of arid land.

More than once Jed Ryland had to turn his head to look back. It was during this that Texas Callahan pulled his trick.

Not for nothing had the tough owl-hoot knocked around the border towns and fought his way from rough-house to ranch.

As Jed Ryland turned his head for a second, Texas acted. His hands left the saddle-horn. He twisted in the saddle. With a terrific push he rammed his weight at Jed Ryland.

Jed was taken unawares and off-balance. In an instant he felt himself slipping. Texas whipped a hand down and grabbed at Jed's right leg. Another heave as the roan galloped on furiously and Jed Ryland was sliding down the rump of the animal.

He hit the ground with a terrible thud. One leg was tangled in the stirrup. For a minute he was dragged along the dusty, shale-covered ground. Then the foot freed. Jed Ryland lay in a huddled heap, his senses momentarily reeling into a black pit.

Texas Callahan, still on the roan, grinned viciously. He shifted himself to the saddle properly and found the stirrups. He grabbed the reins and turned the horse away from the galloping posse.

Only one man saw the whole play. As Texas Callahan wheeled Jed's roan, the posse-man triggered some shots at the outlaw. But owing to the furious galloping of the horse, the shots flew wide. Accurate shooting in such circumstances was almost impossible.

Texas Callahan turned the horse and rode back to join the band of pursuers. He had no guns and could not fire at the lone posse-man who halted his horse and began to ride back for Jed Ryland.

Ezra Strang and the others continued to rowel their mounts over the wasteland. Only one man knew that Jed had taken a severe fall.

Texas Callahan rammed steel-spurred boots cruelly at the roan's flanks. Wide-eyed, the horse pounded on. Texas

141

wheeled it over the wasteland to where Jed Ryland lay. As the horse galloped up Jed stirred and sat up. He was shaking his head like a dog emerging from water. But he was trying to shake off the mists that clouded his brain.

Texas Callahan saw there was a rifle in the saddle holster. But as he cantered up he got a better idea. It was one that appealed to his sadistic mind.

He would use Jed Ryland's own horse to kill him! And Jed would die pretty horribly!

In seconds the roan was close up to the fallen Texas Ranger. Texas Callahan jabbed steel bitingly into the horse's flanks. He reined the animal up, forced the animal to rear its forelegs high in the air.

Then the plunging hoofs beat down— to Jed Ryland's head.

Jed saw the menace. Dazedly, he knew he had not time to get to his feet.

The hoofs were high above his head. Another second and they would ram down.

He rolled clear at the last moment. The horse's hoofs thudded into the dirt. Then Texas Callahan reared the animal again. Hoofs beat wildly at the air as the frightened horse obeyed the cruel jabs which brought blood to its flanks.

Jed rolled desperately for the second time. His face was sweat-streaked and desperate. Texas Callahan wanted him dead. There was a killer lust in the outlaw.

Hoofs thudded harshly into sand and shale inches from Jed's face. As Texas Callahan reared the horse in another vicious attempt at murder, Jed staggered to his feet.

He tried to run. He got five yards away and then he turned and whipped guns from holsters.

Texas Callahan had all the tricks learned through his years on the owl-hoot trail.

The second he saw Jed Ryland could shoot back, he threw himself on the "Injun" side of the roan. Then he urged the horse away.

He was clinging flat to the horse's side. It was an Indian trick. Jed Ryland could not see Texas. He was on the other side of the horse.

With every second that passed Texas Callahan rowelled the horse further away. Jed gritted his teeth. He could not shoot his own horse, and he could not see Texas Callahan. There was only an arm clinging to the roan's neck. To hit that target, on a wildly galloping horse, was next to impossible.

Very quickly Texas Callahan was out of Colt range. He galloped up to the body of outlaws, now pretty close.

Jed could see Krafton Webber at the lead. In spite of his injured shoulder, the owl-hoot boss was riding.

Jed Ryland turned to stumble away. As he turned he saw the lone posse-man riding up. Jed broke into a run to meet the man.

It was a pretty risky job, but the posse-man stuck to his intention. As Jed ran up the man slowed the horse a fraction. Jed vaulted up behind the rider with one leap.

The posse-man applied spurs to the animal, and at headlong lope they went off to join the rest of the posse.

A few shots roared through the air, for the horse with the double load was near enough for a chance shot to bring it down. Jed Ryland was able to turn and loosen off some slugs in retaliation.

There was nothing for the horse with the double load to do but get away. There were six riders in the outfit riding up furiously, now that Texas Callahan had joined them.

Just when it seemed that the double load must be too much for the horse at full lope, the posse with Ezra Strang riding at the head came thundering back. They had noticed that two riders were missing. Hoofs beat an angry tattoo. Ezra still had Andrew Platt up on his cayuse.

Guns began to roar death as the two parties met headlong. Riders kept their mounts at full pace. It was the best way to avoid receiving a Colt slug. But it did not make for good shooting.

For some minutes guns barked and

horsemen raced almost in circles. Then one of the outlaw riders dropped from his horse. He hit the ground and lay still.

The loss of the man evidently decided the other outlaws to break it off. All of a sudden the owl-hoot band rode off and got out of gun range.

Jed Ryland jumped from the posseman's horse and ran to catch the animal that had served the outlaw. The cayuse was a good one, judging by its broad chest, and it was cantering in circles, snorting and eyes wide.

Jed caught it and dragged on the reins. He halted the animal and then vaulted to the saddle. He jigged the mount up to Ezra Strang and the others as they sat on blowing mounts.

"Wal, durn me, I thought you'd stopped a slug!" cried the sheriff. "So we rode back to give yuh a decent burial."

"Kind o' yuh!" jerked the Texas Ranger. He nodded to a distant outcropping of rock around which Krafton Webber and his men had rode. "We're a long way from Monument City, an' those jiggers will follow us and try to dry-gulch us."

"Wal, durn 'em. We got Andrew Platt back safely. Yuh safe now, ain't yuh, Andrew?"

"Safe, heck!" snorted the old-timer. "I ain't bin safe any time in my life! What are we waitin' fer? Let's hit the trail back to our town."

"Shore, Andrew," said Jed Ryland. "We're hittin' the trail. I shore don't like leaving my roan with thet damned hellion, Texas Callahan."

"Mebbe yuh don't," agreed Ezra Strang, "but we got important things at stake—our lives."

The party wheeled horses and began to canter forward. The trail back to Monument was a long, trying one through the broken badlands until they rode down into the valley and the grasslands around the town. They had yet to hit the border, for one thing. They were still in Mexico territory.

"Goshdarn it, yuh shore git handed around, Andrew," joked one posse-man.

147

"First yuh're wi' thet Krafton hombre an' then yuh're back wi' us. Whar d'yuh really wish yuh was, Andrew?"

"Out in the durned desert wi' nuthin' but a burro!" snapped the old fellow.

"Lookin' fer, yore bonanza?" queried the man.

"I don't have to look. I kin go right to it—but no galoot kin foller me. So don't yuh go gittin' ideas."

"We're not interested in yore mine, Andrew," said Jed Ryland. "Leastways, not in any illegal way. I don't suppose the fellers hyar would say no if yuh handed 'em a nugget or two fer savin' yore life."

The bright, beady old eyes glittered.

"Heh! Heh! I might at thet! I ain't promisin'. But I might at thet! Heh! Heh!"

And the old fellow chuckled to himself for the next half hour. Ezra and Jed exchanged glances, amused by the old-timer's craziness. But long years in the desert, looking for elusive bonanzas, had turned Andrew Platt into a queer man indeed.

Presently the old man cackled:

"I shore hope thet gal with me when those hellions started shootin' near my house got away safe. What happened to her? Shore is a nice gal, thet!"

The observation sent a laugh through the jogging riders.

"Yuh got eyes fer a fine wumman!" joked a man.

"Yep. What happened? She's all right, I hope."

"She's back in Monument City," said Jed Ryland. "After the rumpus at yore house, she was taken out as hostage but I caught up with her. Webber killed her father up at the camp. I figger she's hell-bent now to git revenge."

During the talk, and during plenty of other snatches of conversation, Jed Ryland kept a grim outlook for sign of pursuit. But there was no significant dust-cloud on the horizon behind them. This made him think that there would be an attempt to dry-gulch further on. Krafton Webber would not let them take Andrew Platt to safety.

During the last hour the wind had been noticeable. It was increasing in pressure. At first Jed thought it was nothing more than a freshener.

They rode over the border and were back in Texas territory. It was a bit hard to define the border, but by common consent it was a line drawn between two high distant mountains. Further on, about fifty miles, there were other marking features.

"Wal, ef Webber rides across our trail agin," remarked Ezra Strang, "I got power to arrest him. Thet's ef the coyote went suddenly crazy and let me arrest him."

"Why arrest thet hellion?" snapped Andrew Platt. "Ain't he only fitten fer a necktie party?"

"Shore, but I'm a sheriff. I got to arrest and have men tried. Same wi' Jed hyar. He's a Texas Ranger. We got to follow a lawful course."

"Seems like I seed Jed plug thet bartender right between the eyes," remarked Andrew Platt. "Was thet lawful?"

"When another jigger goes fer a gun," said Ezra Strang sternly, "anything's lawful."

The party jogged on through a canyon which gave on to another trail. They stopped at a spring which bubbled from a crack between a pile of rocks. Men drank and filled water canteens. Then the horses muddied the pool with their hoofs and drank notwithstanding. Jed and Ezra kept a wary outlook at the canyon walls. It was a sure thing that enemies were riding around, seeking to find the best spot for attack.

All the time the wind was increasing in pressure. Tiny grains of sand were in the air. The sun became peculiarly red and enlarged. It was an optical illusion, of course. But Jed Ryland, with an expert's eye, saw all the signs of an impending sandstorm.

The others knew it, too. The horses were restless, and after the drink at the spring pool they jogged on with new strength.

The party came out of the canyon. Jed Ryland was riding ahead, with Ezra Strang riding drag on account of the double load.

All at once a rifle cracked and the shell whined through the sombre silence of the evening. The bullet whipped Jed's black hat to the dust. He dug steel at the horse and raced to the shelter of the canyon wall. The other riders streamed after him. Another rifle threw a shot at the party, but because the horses were in full gallop, the bullet went wide.

Then, in a minute, the party of men were sitting saddles and retaining the horses in the shelter of the overhanging canyon wall.

"So them hombres follered us!" rapped Ezra. "Wal, thet was to be expected. Cuss it, if only we had another hoss we could ride for it. This critter is plumb tuckered."

"Let me take Andrew Platt up behind," volunteered a posse-man, a rancher named Tom Burrow. "This hoss o' mine got real guts."

The exchange was made, because the rancher's horse was undoubtedly a magnificent bay with fine stamina.

"Mebbe yuh kin tell me yore little secret now, Andrew?" joked Tom Burrow.

A cackle came from Andrew Platt. He seemed to figure he had the joke of the century.

"Yuh got a mighty fine ranch, Tom Burrow. Yuh don't need no gold. Only old fools like me kin go crazy fer gold. Old fools thet know no other, an' mad coyotes like Webber!"

Some of Webber's outfit had apparently climbed around the mouth of the canyon, for another burst of rifle-fire whined bullets into the walls all around them. It was too close to be comfortable.

Several of the posse-men returned the shots, all to no real effect except to deter the outlaws from coming in any closer.

The sky was a queer reddish hue for miles around. It seemed to have got a lot darker, too. But Jed Ryland knew it was the myriad particles of sand in the air.

In the minutes while the ambushed riders waited, the wind notched up several degrees. The air was filled with a rushing sound. Visibility was less than ten yards or so. Thousands of particles of sand filled the air, stinging the faces of the men and upsetting the horses.

The posse-men tied bandannas around the lower parts of their faces.

With his voice muffled Jed shouted:

"All right. Let's ride on. Those hombres can't see us in this storm. An' by gosh, we can't see them."

In the normal way they would have holed-up against the rocks and waited for the storm to slacken. Sandstorms in those parts were usually of short duration. It might go on for an hour or less.

The riders jogged spooked horses out into the never-ending curtain of sand. They tried to keep together. For some time the animals strained against the storm. The riders kept the horses almost touching each other.

Then one horse slipped a little on some shale that barely covered a hole. With a shrill whinny, the horse nearly stumbled. The rider dragged the animal up almost by the reins. But the damage had been done.

The sudden plunging of the animal caused the others to crow-hop a little. In seconds the riders were parted. Jed Ryland thought he saw a rider and horse in the driving screen of yellow sand. He jigged his animal nearer. But he found he was still no closer. The other rider had moved elsewhere.

As the minutes passed Jed realised the whole party had dispersed. The men could be within yards of each other and yet pass by ignorant of the other's presence.

He cursed the storm. That was unavailing, and did no good except relieve his feelings.

He kept the cayuse plodding on. There was nothing else to do. Everything had gone bad, but perhaps the posse might get together when the storm blew over.

Maybe they should have stayed holed-up against the canyon wall, but that would have found Webber's outfit in front of them just the same when the storm disappeared.

Jed jigged the horse up to some giant boulders. He did not recognise them as part of the trail, but that was nothing. He could be anywhere. He halted the horse in the comparative shelter of the boulder and waited, thoughtfully.

He certainly wished the posse had stayed in the shelter of the canyon wall, but at the time it had seemed a good idea to get as far away from the dry-gulching outlaws as possible.

Jed Ryland dismounted, kept a tight grip on the reins. It would be too bad if the horse spooked and left him. He hugged the side of the big boulder and just waited.

Wind howled like a giant organ, driving sand past the rocky outcrops with a melancholy wail. All around there was nothing but the stinging yellow curtain. Even the red sun was blotted out.

Jed was forced to keep his head down but all the same he kept a sharp look-out. He was peering grimly into the driving sand when a horse with two riders loomed out of the yellow gloom. The cayuse was plodding on against the storm. Another few seconds and the horse and riders would be past, lurching into the blinding storm.

Jed ran out, calling to the man.

"Tom Burrow! Andrew Platt! Hey!"

He staggered up, fighting the pressure of wind. He reached out and slapped the leg of the rider sitting almost on the rump of the animal.

The man turned his face. Jed Ryland received a shock almost as violent as the wind which buffeted him.

In spite of the tied bandanna, he recognised the man as Chub Negler, the hairy gunhawk. He was holding Andrew Platt in front of him on his saddle.

With the recognition, Jed Ryland threw himself into violent attack on the man. He did not know what had happened to Tom Burrow, but he feared the worst.

Jed Ryland grabbed at Chub Negler's leg and hauled. The man slid off the horse in one abrupt movement. As he hit the desert Jed Ryland lurched out grimly to grab at the horse's reins. But the animal, already scared with the storm, leaped away into the sand-filled gloom. Jed made one last frantic effort to grab at the horse. His fingers missed the animal's tail by inches. He saw Andrew Platt trying vainly to control the spooked cayuse. Then, the next instant, gloom swallowed the animal.

Jed Ryland cursed his bad luck and the extraordinary events that were going on. Then, realising that Chub Negler was near by, he wheeled.

Jed staggered forward a few steps and saw the outline of the boulder again. He could not see the horse he had left. There was no sign of Chub Negler.

A few more steps brought him right up to the rock. He put out a hand and felt his way around the outcrop. All at once he blundered into the cayuse, still standing close to the rock wall, its ears pricked back. He grabbed at the animal and soothed it with a few patted strokes of the hand.

He turned as a man lurched grotesquely out of the yellow screen of sand. A gun flashed to Jed's hand. He did not shoot. The other man had his head down against the howling storm and had not seen him and the horse.

In this way the man blundered right up to Jed Ryland, and the Texas Ranger held his fire because he could not be sure of the man's identity.

As the man came within arm's length, Jed saw it was Chub Negler. He had figured it might be that hombre.

Jed slid into rapid action. He slipped his hardware to leather, and then reached out to grab at his man. He coiled a steely arm around the other man's neck even as the other reacted by reaching for guns. Jed slammed a wicked fist down in a chopping motion and knocked two guns right out of the man's hands in a flash. Chub Negler snarled like an animal and jerked backwards in an effort to escape.

"Yuh ain't goin' anywhere!" gritted Jed

Ryland under his breath. "I aim to give yuh a hiding, damn blast yuh!"

It was just the way he felt.

He still had an arm coiled around the outlaw's neck. He jerked the man back and then slammed a haymaker to the man's jaw with his other fist.

Chub Negler fell back under the terrific impact. He fell from Jed's grip. Jed did not mind. He lurched through the furious wind and steadied his feet for the launching of another series of blows.

Chub Negler, without guns, had to face up to the attack. He was a hard-bitten rannigan with a mangy temper in any case. He realised he was left in the storm without a horse or guns. He had seen Jed's animal standing patiently by the rock.

It surged through his mind that he could help himself to the horse and guns if he could beat Jed Ryland.

Actually, he had little choice but fight, for Jed was forcing the showdown on him.

Jed rammed out two wicked hooks—a

right and then a left. The right connected, but as Chub Negler lurched, the left whistled by the man's ear. Then Jed was closer to the owl-hoot.

But Chub Negler figured on dirty tricks. He was fighting for his life, he reckoned, and anything was in order to a desperate man.

He dropped suddenly, helped on by a real stagger as Jed clipped one to the body.

He clawed for a chunk of rock. His hands gripped a bit of shale big as an Irishman's fist. He leaped up again to meet Jed Ryland. The piece of rock left his hand and flew straight for Jed's head.

It was shale, which was good for Jed Ryland.

The rock connected on the Ranger's forehead. It broke into fragments. Bits of chips flew at his eyes. Jed was momentarily blinded. Blood trickled down his forehead.

At the impact, he felt a million shooting lights tear at his senses. He lurched like a sick man. His hands were just splayed forward helplessly. He could not see anything for darkness washed through his mind.

The howl of the wind was added to by a roaring sound in his brain. He staggered and felt himself falling.

The next instant he was clawing at sand. He knew he was sprawling on the desert. He gasped for air, and sand filled his mouth. He fought grimly to beat down the dazedness in his mind.

Chub Negler stood over Jed and figured to kick the Ranger. He brought his boot back and then rammed it at Jed's back. The kick almost rolled over the dazed man.

Chub figured he could kick a man to death if he wanted. Grinning viciously under the bandanna, he brought his foot back for another kick.

Jed Ryland burst through the curtain of dizziness by a terrific effort. He absolutely forced the nausea back. He willed his brain to clear thinking and quick re-action again.

He was still sprawled on the desert

sand. He saw Chub Negler drawing back to administer another savage kick.

Jed Ryland thrust out a hand. He gripped the other man's foot. He made a super effort and heaved back. As he felt the other man stagger, he used his body weight to yank Chub Negler's foot right back.

The man toppled like a pole-axed steer. He thudded into the sand. Jed drove himself on desperately. He dived over the man, raised a bunched fist. He plunged it down, through Chub Negler's threshing fists. Jed's fist rammed home to the other's chin. Jed raised the fist again and plunged it down like a steam hammer.

He did that about five times in succession, and with each blow Chub Negler sagged more and more. The man rasped horribly for breath, sucking in sand. His bandanna had slipped down to his neck. What with the blows and the driving sand which continued to howl like a fury around them, he was almost in danger of choking.

Then Jed Ryland hauled the man up.

They were both in a sitting position. Jed brought out a gun and thumbed the hammer back. He pointed it at Chub Negler.

"All right, feller, the fight's over. I jest figgered to hand out a bit o' punishment. I'm rememberin' you and yore podners cut at Andrew Platt's arms. Git up. Stay quiet or this gun might go off."

Jed hauled the man back to the big boulder. Fortunately the fight had not taken them too far away from the rock. The horse was still there, using its sense and keeping to the shelter. Jed soothed it again. The cayuse seemed glad he was back.

The two men and the animal bunched together against the big boulder. For Chub Negler there was no alternative. He had taken a beating, and now he was on the wrong end of a gun. For Jed Ryland there was constant vigilance, for he knew the gunhawk was full of tricks. Jed's head ached. Blood was a sticky patch on his forehead. He had lost his hat. The sand drove against his unprotected head, stinging the wound. There was still a residue of sickness in his head and a heck of a lot of pains, but he grimly endured all that.

After a long wait in the shelter of the rock he sensed a slackening in the wind pressure. The whining sound was less pronounced. The light seemed a degree brighter. He saw all the signs that the storm was blowing out. The sandstorms were always fast and furious, but they blew over quickly.

It was easier to speak, and he snapped the question he had wanted to ask since he had captured Chub Negler.

"What happened to Tom Burrow? How'd yuh git hold o' Andrew Platt?"

There was no real answer from the gunhawk—just a defiant snarl. Jed prodded the man with the gun.

"Shore, I guess it's a fool question! Yuh must ha got up to Tom Burrow and overpowered him or killed him. Then yuh figgered to git Andrew Platt away, but yuh rode into me. Trouble is, where the blazes is thet old-timer now?"

There could be no answer until the storm passed away and there was some visibility. It was extraordinary to think that in calm weather a man could see for miles in the vast silent wastes, but during a storm all reality was confined to a few yards of blinding sand.

With incredible swiftness, the storm passed away. The transition was almost magical. The pressure of the wind dropped to nil. Sand ceased to blow and pile in queer drifts. The sun was visible as a huge red ball low on the horizon. Although the storm had vanished, sundown was close to hand and that would take its natural course. Jed Ryland figured he had to find the others before sundown.

Presently he thought he could venture from the boulder. He swung to the saddle and pointed a gun at Chub Negler.

"Yuh kin walk, feller. Go git ahead o' this hoss. In thet direction!"

And Jed stuck a finger to the ridge of sandstone hills ahead. He was getting his bearings. He figured he had in mind the trail back to Monument City. But he was not set on riding back until he had located Ezra Strang and the rest of the posse—not to mention Andrew Platt, the cause of all the trouble.

As he rode on, with Chub Negler stumbling ahead on foot, he stood up in the stirrups and surveyed the land. Already he could see for miles, down the canyon where the posse had traversed and over the wasteland to the hilly country which led to Krafton Webber's one-time hideout.

He saw dark, toy-like figures outlined against the red setting sun. They came riding fast towards him. In a few minutes he realised he had moved into a trap.

The riders bearing down on him were undoubtedly Webber and his cohorts. He recognised Webber at the head, holding the reins with one hand.

Jed Ryland wheeled his horse and tore off for the foothills!

7

JED realised he was a fool to leave Chub Negler to link up with his partners. He should have shot the man before he rode off. But such a cold-blooded task was not for him. There had not been time to hoist the owl-hoot up to the saddle. The man would have struggled, employing delaying tactics. Jed thought he would catch up with Chub Negler and the other renegades some day. In the meantime flight was the only course. The outfit behind him numbered six to one. He could not swap lead with those odds.

The main task was to ensure that Andrew Platt was safe. Just where was the old man?

A few shots sped after Jed Ryland, but, curiously, the outlaw band did not pursue any more after they had picked up Chub Negler. Jed reached the first gully in the hilly land and rode out of sight of the outlaws. He jigged the horse up towards a crag at the crest of a shale slope. He wanted a view of the territory before night blanketed down.

Carefully, Jed Ryland rode the animal to the hill and sat tall in the saddle staring around.

He saw a bunch of riders moving fast back in the direction of El Grande. They were indistinguishable dark shapes, and he could not be sure who they were. But he had a hunch the outfit was Webber and his men. He wondered why they were hitting the trail for the Mexican town.

He stared with narrowed eyes at the bunch until they were mere specks on the distant, red horizon. He felt pretty grim about everything. There was a reason why Krafton Webber was heading back to El Grande. There must be a good reason. Could it be that the man had caught Andrew Platt again?

It seemed darned like it. Webber would not let up as long as he had got the old-timer in his power.

With tight lips Jed stared around from the rocky height. All at once he sighted another bunch of riders as they emerged from a shallow ravine about half a mile away. Staring keenly, he guessed he was looking at Ezra Strang and the rest of the posse.

He urged his horse down the shale slope with a slithering of hoofs. He rounded more jutting sandstone outcrops and then found a clear way down to the ravine.

As Jed Ryland rode up, the other riders halted their mounts. Ezra Strang was the first to wave. Jed came up at full lope, and then reined the cayuse with a slithering of hoofs that raised dust.

"Whar's Andrew Platt?" was his first question.

He could see the old-timer was not present—and neither was Tom Burrow nor his fine horse.

"Thet's what we'd like to know," snapped Ezra. "We've had a durned good looksee, but we can't sight Tom Burrow an' thet old jigger wi' him."

Ezra Strang did not know what had happened during the sandstorm.

"I don't figger Andrew Platt will be with Tom Burrow," said Jed grimly. "I had a fight wi' Chub Negler in the blow."

Ezra stared at the red mess on Jed's forehead.

"Yuh shore look like yuh had trouble. What happened?"

"Chub Negler rode up in the storm with Andrew Platt as extra load. I got thet gun-slinger out o' the saddle, but Andrew Platt jest rode off. His hoss was spooked, I guess. Then Chub Negler tried to hammer my head in. Wal, I got over thet. When the storm was over, I almost rode into Webber again. I had to let Chub go. Then I sees Webber an' his rannigans ride off for El Grande."

The sheriff of Monument City fingered his bristling moustache.

"Tarnation! Ef thet hombre, Chub Negler, has killed Tom Burrow, I'll never rest till I got him strung up!"

"I don't like the look of it," muttered Jed.

Ezra braced his shoulders.

"What about it, fellers? Do we ride back to El Grande? Yuh're all sworn in posse-men, but yuh kin back out if yuh want."

The angry growls which greeted the sheriff's remarks decided everything.

"All right!" roared Ezra. "We're agoin' back to thet durned town."

"We'll git Andrew Platt or bust!" bawled one man.

"Ef thet old jigger would only file claim on thet bonanza," snapped another man, "he'd git real protection. Ef Webber or any other hombre tried to jump the claim, Andrew Platt c'd ha' a whole passel o' Texas Rangers shootin' them fellers off afore they got an ounce o' gold out of the mine. Yes, sir! Gold is jest as valuable to the State as to any jigger, an' the authorities would step in and stop fellers like Webber. But thet old idjut won't even file claim. Shore ain't no wonder he got hombres after his durned gold!"

There were grim smiles at the outburst. The men knew it was perfectly true, but

172

that did not alter the fact that Andrew Platt had to be rescued. Ezra Strang was sheriff of Monument City, and Andrew Platt was a citizen of that worthy town. Jed Ryland had been sent to help Ezra clear up the outlaw band. He had arrived just when Webber had thought of his plan to get the old-timer's secret bonanza.

It was many hours later when the bunch of tired riders entered El Grande again. It was dark, with a pale moon casting an eerie light over the desert. Desert nights could be mysterious and fascinating, but to the posse rest and food was a stronger attraction.

They had no plans. There were, for one thing, out of their territory. Theoretically, Krafton Webber, with Chub Negler and Texas Callahan and the rest of the bunch, were immune from Texas law. Only with the co-operation of Jose Petrillio could anything be done against them. That co-operation would not be forthcoming.

Ezra Strang took his tired men into the nearest saloon and bought them drinks.

After two shots of red-eye, the men began to be a bit more cheerful.

Jed was grim and restless. He went around to the back of the saloon and got some water from a half-breed server. He sluiced blood and dust from his head. He felt a lot better. He came back to Sheriff Strang.

"You an' me are goin' on a prowl around this burg," he said. "I figger two kin find out just as much as a posse."

"Shore, let's go git thet old galoot. Whar do we look first?"

"Right in the Santa Alicia," returned Jed.

"Mebbe they got a new hooch slinger, huh?"

"Could be. The other gink wouldn't be much use. Ef anyone gits in my way, there'll be trouble!"

Jed Ryland was in a new mood. For the time being, he wanted to act as if he was not a Texas Ranger and a law-man. He was grimly determined to force a showdown. He could not help but remember the red cuts on Andrew Platt's arms. Maybe right now, Krafton Webber was inflicting new torture in an effort to make the old-timer speak.

Jed and Ezra strode into the bar-room of the Santa Alicia. Sure enough there was a new bartender, with three half-breed servers to assist because it was a busy time. Ezra and Jed eased up to the counter and ordered rye.

They had hardly got the drinks when Jose Petrillio lounged up. His bulky stomach was covered by a flowered vest, now that it was night and a lot cooler. He wore his store suit. He had rings on his fingers, and the two guns slung low against his thighs. The long-tailed coat almost obscured the holsters.

"Howdy," said Ezra Strang. "Yuh seen anything of them hombres we was talking about?"

It was, of course, an idle question and Ezra knew it. Jose Petrillio merely smiled. His swarthy face creased expansively.

"Howdy, amigos. You still look for these bad mens? I do not think you will find them in this cantina."

Jed Ryland moved his head and stared deliberately at the balcony at the end of the long bar-room.

"Mebbe yuh would like to let us take a pasea at the rooms upstairs?"

Sheriff Petrillio rolled his eyes.

"Señors, this is a fine saloon. Only the best people ever stay at my cantina. I do not like shooting. No, I am so sorree, but there is no need for you to look into the rooms of this cantina."

"Look, yuh let rooms to Krafton Webber when they rode in early this day," snapped Jed. "Let's forgit the oily talk, amigo. I found an old coot name o' Andrew Platt upstairs some hours ago. He was well hog-tied, but I got him free. Some ginks had been workin' on him, if yuh interested. Yuh know durned fine I had to shoot a way out o' this joint. Now what about takin' us up and showing us around like a real pard?"

"That I cannot allow." said Jose Petrillio smoothly. "I have guests staying in the rooms above this cantina. I have wealthy Mexican ranchers stay here, señor. They must not be disturbed. You understand?"

"Yep, we understand!" growled Ezra Strang.

He exchanged glances with Jed Ryland. Jose Petrillio was a bit reluctant to let them look over the cantina. It was not because of his important guests. Important ranchers who stayed at the Santa Alicia were probably few and far between. No. Jose Petrillio was trying to stop them from looking around.

"Okay, Sheriff Petrillio," said Jed Ryland swiftly. "We're law-men. We won't create any disturbance. Guess we'll shayshay along and see if we kin lamp those hombres. We figger they're in El Grande somewheres."

They knocked back the red-eye which had been served them for whisky and walked through the arguing and gesticulating crowd of vaqueros and white rannigans. They reached the boardwalk outside before Jed said anything. Then:

"Thet oily old buzzard! I got an idee

he's working in with Webber. Shore as heck, he's givin' Webber room."

"Yuh got any idees, young feller?" asked Ezra.

"Yep. We kin do what I did the last time."

Jed Ryland led the way around to the back of the place. They began climbing the posts that supported the veranda. Jed was first up and he gave Ezra Strang a hand.

"Danged ef I'm as young as you!" breathed Ezra.

They were on the veranda and outside the windows. Jed went straight to the one behind which he had found Andrew Platt earlier in the day. The window was covered with a blind. He tried the frame and found it moved.

Jed pushed the window up softly. He pulled the blind to one side and stared into a darkened room.

He did not expect to find Andrew Platt sitting in the room bound to a chair once more. That was expecting too much, he felt.

"Let's git inside this place," he whispered to Ezra. "Shucks to thet Jose Petrillio. We kin take a look around and then calmly walk out, if we find nothing."

With a minimum of noise, they put boots over the window-sill and climbed into the room. For a second or two they stood in the dark, then they walked quietly to the door.

Jed was first to reach the door. He put a hand on the knob. He was aware of Ezra close behind him. He began to turn the knob.

Swiftly, something moved close by in the darkness. In a flash, a gun-barrel rammed wickedly at his heart.

"Don't move, hombre!" said a voice.

Ezra Strang stiffened as if every muscle in his body had gone taut. A gun had rammed into his back simultaneously with the threat to Jed.

A match spluttered and yellow light flared around the room.

The scene was grim enough. Jed and Ezra had walked right into a trap, and Jose Petrillio had had a say in it.

Krafton Webber held a Colt on Jed Ryland. A false move and a slug would crash out of the snout of the gun and bring instant death. There was no doubt about that.

Texas Callahan stood behind Ezra and held a gun at the sheriff. It was a grim, taut moment. Thin, wary grins were on the lips of Webber and Texas Callahan. Chub Negler stood with the match and lit an oil-lamp. The yellow gleam illuminated the whole room in a second. The lamp was still hot, proving that it had been put out just before the men positioned themselves.

"Howdy, hombres," sneered Krafton Webber. "Yuh lookin' fer somethin'?"

There was a snicker from Texas and Chub Negler.

"Maybe yuh lookin' fer gold!" went on Webber, and he laughed again sneeringly.

Slowly, Jed straightened. His hands were halfway up. To drop them would invite a bullet.

Ezra Strang thought he could relax a bit, too. He turned and faced Texas

Callahan. He kept his hands shoulder high.

"Jose tell yuh to expect us?" snapped Jed.

Krafton Webber nodded his head, his big red cheeks having a triumphant expression.

"He shore did. Jose Petrillio is a mighty handy feller to know. He told us yuh were in town and nosing around the bar downstairs. We came into this room an' heard yuh climbin' the veranda. Yuh shore don't move like Injuns!"

"Wal, yuh got the drop on us!" snapped Ezra. "What yuh figger to do wi' us? Yuh intend to stand hyar all night yapping?"

Krafton Webber turned glinting eyes to Chub Negler.

"Git thar guns."

Texas Callahan kept his shooting iron right into the middle of Ezra Strang. Webber never took his eyes from Jed as Chub Negler lifted the hardware from the men's holsters.

"Fine. Now we kin relax," said Krafton Webber.

"Yuh scared we'll eat yuh?" taunted Jed.

Anger glinted in the outlaw boss's eyes.

"Yuh plugged me once, yuh lousy snakeroo!"

Then Krafton Webber seemed to get a grip on his temper.

"All right. I've got plenty o' time to figger out ways o' showing yuh it don't pay to cross me. Now git moving. We happen to have Andrew Platt in another room."

"Made him talk yet?" rapped Jed.

"Nope. He's an obstinate cuss. An' we got to treat him gently. We shore don't want him to git badly hurt. He's got to ride with us when he gives us directions to find thet bonanza. He's a tricky hombre."

"He'll trick yuh yet," taunted Jed.

He had no other weapon he could use at the moment. It pleased him to make Krafton Webber mad with rage.

"This time we're gittin' thet gold!"

hissed the man. "We're making Platt give directions to-night. We don't aim to waste any more time. To-morrow we hit the trail fer thet gold!"

Under the menace of two guns, there was nothing else for Ezra and Jed to do but walk through the door which Chub Negler opened. At least they were still alive. Webber seemed to have the idea he had time in which to kill them.

They were pushed down another passage to a mahogany door which Chub Negler unlocked with a key which Webber gave him. Another second and the party were inside the hotel room.

As Jed had expected, old Andrew Platt was bound to a chair. But his hands were not tied behind his back.

The old-timer's feet were well hog-tied, but his arms were strapped down along the arms of the cane chair.

The old fellow's hands were immovable. Jed's eyes narrowed grimly as he saw the flecks of red blood at the tips. Then he realised the terrible torture that Webber was employing.

At the end of Andrew Platt's finger-nails, sharp splinters of wood protruded. Webber had been using some outlandish torture to make the old man talk. He had driven the splinters into Andrew Platt's fingers, under the nails. It was a wonder the old man had suffered the torture without breaking.

"Jest sit down and see how we kin work, Ryland," said Webber. "Mebbe yuh kin figger what will come to you. I ain't forgottin' yuh're a double-crossing snake."

"If yuh want to know," said Jed quietly. "I'm a Texas Ranger, sent to help Sheriff Strang clean yuh out o' Monument City territory."

"Is that so?" sneered the boss. "Wal, I had figgered somethin' like thet. We're out o' Monument City now, ain't we? This is Mexico. But forgit it. How'd yuh like to hear Platt tell everybody whar to find his bonanza?"

With Chub Negler and Texas Callahan holding guns on Ezra and Jed, Webber

184

started to inflict more torture on Andrew Platt.

His first action was to undo the gag which was wrapped around the miner's mouth.

"Thet's so yuh kin talk, Andrew!" sneered Webber. "I shore don't want to stop yuh from talkin'! I only put the gag on tuh keep yore trap shut while we were out o' the room!"

Andrew Platt gave vent to a moan, but that was all.

"Yuh'll say more'n thet!" snarled Webber.

He drove another splinter of wood under the old-timer's finger-nail. The oldster's hand was bound firmly to the chair, and although he squirmed like a trapped animal, the ropes did not give. A shuddering cry broke from Andrew Platt's lips. His eyes rolled desperately and sweat trickled all over his face. His white stubble was dirty with sweat and dust.

"Where's the location?" hissed Webber. "Speak, yuh blamed fool? I mean to have it! An' tell the truth! If yuh lie to me, I'll cut yuh into ribbons when we git out into the badlands and find yuh're foolin'!"

Jed Ryland itched to jump to his feet and start a shindy. That was, of course, the quickest way to boothill. Chub Negler would take the opportunity to blast him. The man was longing to do that, in any case, after the beating Jed had given him in the sandstorm.

Ezra Strang sat foaming. His instinct was to start anything that would give a chance. But nothing was of avail against a menacing gun. These gunhawks probably meant to blast them sooner or later . . .

Krafton Webber drove two of the splinters deeper into flesh. Andrew Platt's body writhed in the bonds. Moans escaped his lips.

"Talk, durn yuh! Whar's the location o' thet gold? Yuh hear me? Talk! Talk!"

With the ruthless words, Webber applied more force to the torture splinters. A shrill scream of pure agony burst from the old-timer's twisted lips.

"Talk! Talk! Talk!"

It was more than human nature could stand. Jed Ryland felt sick. He had seen Indian torture, and this was pretty near to it. Suddenly a torrent of words burst from the old-timer's lips. It was like a log-jam breaking free. The oldster babbled about the mine and alternately pleaded with Webber to take the torture splinters out of his fingers.

With sudden greed glinting in his eyes, Krafton Webber leaned forward as if he would get the sense of the flow of words. He pulled the splinters out and threw them to the floor. It was nothing to him. He could start the whole thing over again if Andrew Platt was fooling.

But the oldster was broken. He babbled something about the Guadalupes, near the Texas-Mexico border. Webber slapped his face brutally.

"Take it easy, yuh old fool! Now whar's the location?"

"Guadalupe Mountains . . . in a canyon . . ."

"Yep? Wal, thet ain't no use. Them blastit mountains stretch for miles."

"Hell-country!" snapped Texas Callahan. "A jigger kin die up in those hills. No water, nuthin' but rattlers and desert and peaks stretching right up into the sky. He's got to tell us jest whar the bonanza is!"

"He'll tell," rapped Webber.

He slapped Andrew Platt back to reality. The old fellow had gone into a daze with the reaction from the agony.

"Whar's the canyon? How'd we git up thar? How many miles is it?"

"Fifty miles from Monument . . . due west," gasped Andrew Platt. "Then take old Indian trail through twin peaks. Then I hev to lead the burro over a canyon ten miles long. At the end, yuh come acrosst the bonanza."

"Yeah? Jest whar is the bonanza?"

"It's jest a kinda cleft in the rocky floor o' the canyon," whispered Andrew Platt. "I guess no one c'd find it ef they didn't know jest exactly whar to look. Thet cleft has bin there fer hundreds o' years . . .

jest full o' gold . . . yuh only got to shovel it up . . . pure nuggets. I reckon there's a seam, but I ain't never bothered to dig."

Greed glittered in Krafton Webber's dark eyes. Already he thought he could see the unlimited wealth. If it was as rich as Andrew Platt described, there was gold to make all his outfit rich for life. They could take it easy in some lawless town. Money would buy everything, even security.

"All right, hombre!" breathed Krafton Webber. "Yuh kin draw us a map. An' make it right or yuh'll git some more splinters in yore fingers."

"Guadalupes!" muttered Texas Callahan. "Thet durned range has killed hundreds! It's jest a waterless waste an' a jigger kin git lost and wander around until his water gives out. Nary a damned soul fer hundreds o' miles. Nuthin' but vultures and eagles. I've heerd about it!"

"Shut yore durned mouth!" snapped Webber. "Ef yuh figger it's too tough for yuh, wal, I guess yuh kin light out."

"I'm not lighting out!" snarled Texas Callahan.

"Wal, for gawd's sake shut up an' help me git the ropes offen this feller. Treat him easy. He may be still foolin'. He's got to show us this cleft in the Guadalupes, remember."

Although Texas Callahan helped Krafton Webber to undo the ropes binding the oldster, Chub Negler kept a wary gun on Jed and Ezra.

For a moment Jed Ryland thought this was the only chance they would ever get of jumping the outlaws. Mebbe he could draw the fire, and mebbe Ezra would get hold of a gun . . .

And then he knew it was utterly impossible in face of Chub Negler's gun. The bearded gun-slinger was watching them intently. He could pump slugs into them before they moved more than six inches.

Krafton Webber brought out from his pocket a sheet of paper and a pencil. He stuck them in front of Andrew Platt when they got the oldster to the small table.

"Git drawin' thet map! We want it in case anythin' should happen to yuh. Make the map right or by thunder it will be the worse for yuh later on when we find out it's a trick."

"I don't aim to trick yuh!" muttered Andrew Platt, as he bent his white head over the paper. "I'll draw yuh a good map, gents. Yuh kin find the gold by it yoreself. Ef yuh read it a-right yuh don't need me up thar. I'm an old galoot an' I don't want to make any more trips into thet durned wilderness. I got all the gold tuh last me. Yuh don't really need me up thar with yuh."

Krafton Webber was no fool. He had been trained for better things before taking to a life of lawlessness. He exchanged glances with Texas Callahan, and then turned ugly eyes on Andrew Platt.

"Who the heck d'yuh figger yuh're foolin'? Yuh c'd draw a fool map. Nope! Yuh goin' up thar with the outfit to-morrow. We'll git a start at sun-up. I got the rannigans out now buyin' hosses and grubstakes. Keeps them busy. Draw thet map, hombre, an' make it good. An' remember yuh're goin' with us, so the map had better be right."

With a groan, the old-timer realised he was beaten. With a gesture of resignation he held the pencil in his numbed fingers and began to draw laboriously.

His efforts attracted the attention of Texas Callahan as if he would memorise the map for himself. Even Chub Negler was giving glances at Andrew Platt as time went on.

It was very silent in the room. There was only the old fellow's laboured breathing and an occasional grunt of satisfaction from Krafton Webber.

Wary as an animal fighting for survival, Jed Ryland watched the movements of Chub Negler's head. The man was the only one holding a gun on them at the moment. True, Texas Callahan and Krafton Webber had guns in their holsters—Texas had apparently retrieved his hardware from Andrew Platt—and they could withdraw at the speed of light.

After some ten minutes of slow draughtsmanship, Andrew Platt finished the map. He put the pencil down slowly. He stared at his fingers, and then looked at Krafton Webber.

"I shore hope the Guadalupes git yuh!" he hissed. "An' ef I'm wi' yuh when yuh go mad with thirst, I'll jest laugh an' laugh! Mebbe the Guadalupes will git me, but if they do they'll shore git yuh, hombre!"

An ugly twist came to Webber's mouth. He nearly slammed a hand at the old-timer's head. But he stopped after the initial movement.

"We got to keep yuh healthy, podner!" he sneered. "Yuh're goin' to act as guide to the gold."

Krafton Webber picked up the map, stared at it.

"Mighty nice," he was sneering.

The door slammed open with terrific force. A man stood in the doorway and thumbed the hammer of a gun.

As the hogleg roared, men dived for cover. Chub Negler rammed back under the impact of a .45 slug in his chest. The gun fell from his hand. The next second a Colt roared from the window, shattering glass and bursting the oil-lamp to bits!

The lamp toppled over and was extinguished in a second. All around was confusion and shooting. Guns flashed from the window and the door. Men were taking cover behind the door and window. And shots were tearing from Krafton Webber's gun to the window. Someone else was shooting at the door.

The room was pretty big and it was dark except for the gun-flashes.

Jed was on the floor. He knew Ezra Strang had dived flat the moment the man in the doorway had shot. Chub Negler was dead, he guessed.

Jed knew the man at the door was one of the posse-men. He felt a great exultation at the thought they might beat Webber yet. The man at the window, on the veranda, must surely be one of Ezra's men, too. Jed could not see him. Maybe there was more than one man outside.

Noticing how long Ezra and Jed had been away, the posse-men had acted . . .

A gun blazed from a corner of the room and Jed got a momentary glimpse of Webber's savage face by the light of the gun-flash. The slug did not come anywhere near Jed, so he figured Krafton Webber was shooting elsewhere.

In that moment Jed Ryland wished he had a gun. But they had been taken from him. He wondered where Ezra was lying. He was not far away. But to move would attract attention.

All at once a burst of concentrated shooting at the doorway forced the posse-man to dash back. He seemed to get back to a corner of the passage. The two outlaws in the room leaped to the door and jumped out into the passage. They wanted to be out of the room and the cross-fire.

Jed stumbled around the room and nearly fell over a body. He bent down and knew by the hairy visage that he had found Chub Negler. Quickly, he got the man's two guns. As he moved, a match flared. Ezra was holding it. Jed stared around by the light and saw that Andrew Platt had stopped a slug. He was lying in a huddle, with a hole in his head.

Jed wasted no time on useless staring. He thrust a gun into Ezra Strang's hand.

At the same time a posse-man climbed through the broken window. He had a smoking hogleg in his hand. Jed jerked his head to the man and together the three moved to the doorway.

They saw Krafton Webber and Texas Callahan throwing lead from a corner at the extreme end of the passage. Both men were not showing much beyond a rapidly thrusting hand holding a gun.

Jed and Ezra, with the other posse-man, began throwing lead. And then Jed Ryland realised they had to get out of the Santa Alicia. Men were coming up the staircase. They would be either the other outlaws or Jose Petrillio's vaqueros.

The posse-man at the head of the passage darted back with Jed and Ezra to the room which had just recently seen the fighting. Together the four men dashed to the window.

Jed Ryland passed the dead old-timer and picked him up. There was nothing he could do for Andrew Platt. The old gent would never see gold any more. Rapidly, because there was not time to lose, Jed moved to the window. He did not stop to examine Andrew Platt. He knew he was dead. He had stopped a slug in the shooting.

Only one man had got through to the door of the room. The other posse-men were still on the veranda. One man had slipped up the stairway when no one was looking. He had got to the door and listened long enough to realise what was going on. At the same time, the other posse-men had been on the veranda wondering which window might be the best to tackle. While they had been there the shooting had started. So they had thrown their share of lead from the window.

In seconds, the men descended from the veranda by means of climbing in the

197

approved way. Andrew Platt was handed down, and then the outfit ran off into the darkness of the alley. They were making for the horses.

Chub Negler was dead, but Krafton Webber and Texas Callahan were still alive and dangerous. Worse, although Andrew Platt was dead, Webber had a plan showing the location of the bonanza. To a certain extent, he had succeeded so far.

At the head of the men who climbed the stairs was Jose Petrillio. He walked into the room. A vaquero handed him a lamp. Jose looked around and then stopped swiftly to bend down and pick up a crumpled sheet of paper. Without looking at it, Jose Petrillio thrust the paper into his pocket. Not for nothing was he known as a shrewd man in El Grande.

In another second Krafton Webber and Texas Callahan strode into the room. They stared around for sign of Andrew Platt.

Then they looked at the window.

"They've taken the old gink away, doggone 'em!" snapped Krafton Webber.

He did not know that the old gold miner was dead. In the confusion that had reigned, he had known only that there were guns flashing and life was precarious.

Krafton Webber cursed somewhat.

"We'll ha' to git thet old jigger! Maybe I've got the map, but I need him as a guide."

Texas was not listening. He was looking at Chub Negler with grim distaste. Texas felt that each death brought his own a bit nearer.

Krafton Webber felt for the map which he had thrust into a pocket the moment the shooting had started from the door-way.

He brought out the map and nearly shouted wth rage. He had only one half. The sheet had been torn exactly in half.

Neither Jose Petrillio nor Webber was to know that Andrew Platt had made his last effort to keep his secret. As the shooting started, he had snatched at the map, tearing half away. Then he had been killed. Jed Ryland had not noticed the crumpled sheet fall from Andrew Platt's hand when he had hoisted him up. But, then, the room had been in semi-darkness.

Jose Petrillio watched Krafton Webber shrewdly, and suddenly realised that the sheet of paper he had picked up could be mighty important.

If that was the case he was not the hombre to say anything until he had time to figure out the various angles.

8

THE shooting was over. Silence did not exactly fall over the Santa Alicia, but the hubbub from the bar returned to normal.

Krafton Webber and Texas Callahan had taken their men out to look for the Texan posse-men. Jose Petrillio, sitting in a wide cane chair in his private sitting-room, figured the two parties had not met up because the streets were fairly silent.

He was much more intent upon studying the crumpled sheet of paper which he held carefully. He had been examining it for some time.

He had the map positioned properly because he could read the words: "Guadalupe Mountains" in the top part. And at the bottom, as if giving title to the map, had been some more words. All that was on Jose Petrillio's sheet was the shortened: "-nanza."

Jose Petrillio was nobody's fool. He had a good part of El Grande tied up the way he wanted it, and the cantina paid nicely. He knew mighty fine that the word which had been torn almost in half was "bonanza". Anything in the nature of a bonanza was mighty interesting to Jose Petrillio.

He knew Krafton Webber had some important play on. And the Texan posse-men had told him that Webber's prisoner was rich. This added up. A bonanza, in these parts, meant gold. Webber was after gold. The shooting parley was over gold.

Jose Petrillio had noticed Krafton Webber's rage as he stared at his torn sheet of paper. At the time Jose had not known the actual importance of the paper. Now he did.

Somehow, in the rumpus, the map to a gold bonanza had been torn in half. Webber had one half. He was filled with ungodly rage because the map had been torn.

Jose Petrillio, by the Saints' good graces, had the other half. That was verree interesting. But half a map was not much use. A man could not travel by half a map.

Jose Petrillio rose and tucked the piece of paper very carefully into a secret pouch in his belt.

He went to a window and stared out into the night. There seemed to be no shooting in the streets of El Grande.

He prepared to go down to the saloon and wait events.

Krafton Webber and Texas Callahan, with the remainder of their owl-hoot band, returned to the Santa Alicia saloon in a disgruntled mood. They had searched the streets of the town for sign of the Texan posse only to realise the horses were not at any tie-rail. It was evident that Ezra Strang had ridden out with his men.

"Goldarn it, we got to git hittin' the trail again!" snarled Webber. "My damned shoulder hurts like hell! But we got to git after them hellions. They've got

Andrew Platt. In fact, it's worse than that."

"Can't we make out wi' the map?" asked Texas Callahan.

Krafton Webber was under the impression that Andrew Platt had been rescued alive. He had not known that the old-timer had taken a slug during the gun-play.

Texas Callahan was under the impression that Webber had the map intact. Krafton Webber, consumed by an in-bitten rage, figured to open his side-kick's eyes.

He brought out the torn sheet of paper with Andrew Platt's last handiwork scrawled on it.

"Take a pasea at thet!"

Texas narrowed his black eyes and stared.

"The durned thing's torn!"

"Yuh said it, pal! It got torn in half during thet blastit gun-play."

"How?"

Krafton Webber had figured it all out. "I guess thet durned old mangy desert rat grabbed at the map jest as thet shootin' started. Andrew Platt has the other half o' the map, blast him! And thet old idjut is ridin' back wi' Ezra Strang and thet blamed Ranger. C'mon! Git those hombres to leather! We got to git ridin' again."

"Hell, I'm mighty tired o' ridin'!" snarled Texas Callahan. "Awright, I'll git them hombres to leather."

"We know they've hit back fer Monument City, anyways," snapped Webber. He put a hand up and held his shoulder. He seemed to be feeling pain in the bullet wound. "Goldarn it! Ef ever I git a hogleg on those fellers, I'll shoot fust and parley afterwards."

"We oughta filled 'em with lead when we had 'em in the room upstairs," grunted Texas.

"Shore. Now git those range hellions to saddles. Tell 'em we're riding after those Texans. Ain't nuthin' for it but catch up wi' thet party and start shooting. We can't find the bonanza wi' half a map."

Texas Callahan walked away, grousing.

"Cayn't find it mebbe wi' the whole map!" he muttered. "Those damned Guadalupe Mountains is jest a wilderness o' burning sun and wasteland. Thet territory kilt many a desert tramp—gents thet know the land. Ef we git gold out o' thar, we'll be mighty lucky!"

He passed Jose Petrillio standing by the bar. The sheriff smiled greasily at him. Jose Petrillio waited until Krafton Webber strolled up.

"You pay for damage, huh?" questioned the sheriff.

"What blamed damage?"

"Windows upstairs and broken chairs," said Jose blandly. "And shooting is not good for reputation."

"We're ridin' out!" snarled Webber. "Mebbe we'll be back, and mebbe we won't. But I allus settle my bills. Hyar!"

He thrust some dirty dollar bills at the Mexican. Jose Petrillio accepted them because he had never been known to pass up money, soiled or otherwise.

"Fer board and rooms!" snarled Webber.

"Gracias! Thank you, Meester Webber. You succeed in making old rannigan talk?"

"Yuh talk, too!" sneered Krafton Webber, and he eased his Colt out of the holster and showed it to the sheriff of El Grande. "Shut yore trap about what goes on wi' me an' mine. Understand? Yuh bin paid fer rooms. Mebbe we ain't a-comin' back. All I kin thank yuh for is warning us about them hellions nosing around hyar lookin' for us. Adios."

As Krafton Webber strode away, Jose Petrillio murmured: "Adios, amigo."

Then he smiled and brought out a long thin cigar and put it in his mouth. As he lit it with a sulphur match he was smiling broadly.

Ezra Strang and Jed Ryland rowelled the horses out of El Grande and took to the trail leading back to Texas territory. Ezra had the body of Andrew Platt slung over the front of his saddle. It was the only way to carry the dead fellow.

They kept the animals at full canter

although the critters were plenty tired. The riders intended to get well away from El Grande and then camp somewhere in the broken lands. They figured to find a hideout for the night and bed down with saddle blankets. The horses could do with the rest. Tomorrow would see them on the trail again.

A moon threw pale light over the desert, revealing clumps of mesquite bush and skeleton-like ocotillo cactus. One of the posse-men, a lean, tall fellow by the name of Hank Carter, began to sing a mournful trail song.

Ezra Strang puckered his nose at the song. He endured it for some time as the bunch cantered ever onward over the undulating stretches of sand and shale. Then Ezra's moustache bristled.

"Fer Pete's sake, turn thet durned dirge off!"

"Shucks, I was only singin'!" protested the posse-man.

"Sounds plenty horrible tuh me!"

"It's an old trail song what my paw useter sing!" muttered Hank Carter.

"Yeah? Yuh're paw's kinda dead, ain't he? Thet durned song sounds like a lament."

Jed Ryland grinned thinly at the back-chat. He knew Ezra Strang was merely barking for the sake of arousing some sort of cheerfulness among the men.

The body slung across his saddle had affected them all. It seemed they had failed to protect Andrew Platt. A chance slug had killed the old-timer. Maybe the shot had emerged from an outlaw gun, but no one knew.

Ezra Strang stood up in the stirrups.

"Ain't so far to thet ridge o' hills. I figger we had best hole-up fer the night."

"Shore. We kin post a guard," said Jed. "I'll do first watch, if yuh like. Webber might ride after us. But thet cuss has the map Andrew Platt made for him. He's more likely to start gettin' ready for a ride to the Guadalupes."

"Blast him!" Ezra Strang swore even more fiercely than that for a whole minute. Then: "We ain't bin so smart, Jed. Thet hombre has a map to the bonanza. Mebbe Andrew Platt is dead, but thet won't stop Webber from goin' prospectin' fer thet gold. And with a map, he'll likely git it!"

"Andrew Platt got any relatives?" inquired Jed.

"None thet I know."

"Because if he has, they've got a right to the map. That map was got from Andrew Platt by force. He didn't give it away, and we were witnesses to thet fact. Ef Webber sets off for the Guadalupes, I got a hanker to go right after him. I don't like the idee o' him gittin' thet gold."

Ezra Strang smoothed the mane of his horse.

"Thet's the only way. I can't ask a posse to ride into them durned mountains. Aw, heck, the gold's up thar and Andrew Platt never filed claim on it. I guess the gold belongs to any feller. And Andrew Platt is plumb dead. Say, we'll ha' to bury him tonight, Jed. Anyways, we kin give him a decent burial, pore gink!"

Jed Ryland nodded grimly, blond hair

falling thickly over his forehead. He was hatless. He had only one gun. Texas Callahan still had his roan. The horse he was riding belonged to the outlaw remuda.

"Shore. Yuh got authority to give a Christian burial, Ezra. Yuh know the words to use. But I ain't forgettin' thet Krafton Webber got no right to thet gold. I'm goin' to have thet map offen him. He ain't got no right to it. If thet hellion kin find the gold without a map, well an' good. But I aim to ride thet cuss to earth."

And Jed Ryland thought grimly on those lines. He could not know that Krafton Webber was far from having possession of the whole map. One, Jose Petrillio, was mighty interested, too.

Jed had memorised Andrew Platt's verbal instructions to Krafton Webber. Jed remembered the old-timer saying:

"Fifty miles from Monument . . . due west . . . Then take old Indian trail through twin peaks. Then I hev to lead the burro over a canyon ten miles long. At the end, yuh come acrosst the bonanza."

Jed recalled the words very clearly. They were burned in his memory.

Anyone following the instructions would get near the location, but it would not be an easy matter finding a cleft in a ten-mile long canyon. It could be done only with the map. Even the canyon might look like other canyons in that arid wilderness. It would be mighty easy to get lost. And to get lost was certain death. There was no water.

So the way Jed Ryland figured it, he could ride back to Monument City with the posse and then get a grubstake and new guns, including a rifle. He'd need a new hat and other gear. A trip to the Guadalupes could not be done without preparation.

But he figured he would track Krafton Webber and his outfit, if they were up in those mountains seeking the bonanza by means of the map. He could track them and then force a showdown.

After some dogged riding, the men reached the sandy gullies of the broken country. After some riding around, they found an ideal spot to make camp. They would not light a fire in case Webber had decided to follow and shoot them up. But there was grass and water from a spring. The horses would rest here.

The weary riders got down from saddles and pulled saddle-bags off the mounts. They unrolled saddle blankets and sat in a circle. Ezra and Hank Carter carried Andrew Platt's body to a crevice and laid it down. The rest of the men came up silently and stood around, bareheaded.

Ezra Strang was, among other things, a preacher in Monument City's church halls.

He began his duty. He repeated part of a burial service. The men stared down at the dead man in the sandy crevice. All around was the utter silence of the desert night. Not even a coyote howled at the moon.

"—May the Almighty have mercy on this old sinner!" concluded Ezra gruffly. Then, in another tone: "All right, men, git some sand an' stones over the body. Ain't fitten thet the buzzards should git Andrew Platt after the desert trampin' he's done!"

A few minutes later it was finished. Large stones were placed in the crevice to stop coyotes from getting at the body. A rough cairn marked the spot as a burial-place.

"All right, let's git bedded down!" snapped Ezra Strang. "Goldarn it, I'm a mighty weary man!"

They walked back to the horses. Saddles had been removed but the reins were still on the animals. With the reins thrown over the horses' heads and wrapped around a chunk of rock, the animals would not stray.

Jed Ryland, true to his word, took on duty as a night hawk.

He stationed himself on a crag of rock. It was utterly silent. He could see a silvery gleam on the wasteland for miles around.

According to his thinking, Krafton Webber would not waste energy in following them for the purpose of shooting it out.

Krafton Webber had the map. To a certain extent he had succeeded so far in his ambitions.

All at once it occurred to Jed Ryland that Webber might not know that Andrew Platt was dead.

Sitting on the rock, Jed scratched his head at this new thought. He went over the action that had taken place in the room at the Santa Alicia. The room had been really dark. The gun-flashes had been blinding. No one had known what was really happening. Then Krafton Webber and Texas Callahan had gotten out of the room and kept up the lead singing from the passage.

It was possible Webber figured the posse had got Andrew Platt away from the cantina alive.

The more Jed thought about it, the more he grew puzzled. In the end, he stopped going over the ideas. If Webber thought Andrew Platt was alive, he might continue to fight to get possession of the old fellow.

Jed smiled grimly. That would be a difficult task. Webber could not do much with a dead man.

He concentrated on turning his head to scan the surrounding desert. It was flattish country ahead. At his back was the broken land, with its rash of rocky outcrops turning the land into a veritable maze.

Just behind him, below in the grassy basin, the posse-men stretched in a well-earned rest. The horses were a dark huddle as they moved occasionally for fresh grass. They would feed and then rest. Horses could take care of themselves!

Some instinctive sense of danger prompted Jed Ryland to snap his head around. He stared keenly over the moonlit wasteland.

About a mile away, on the flat desert country, a few black shapes moved. Jed Ryland kept keen blue eyes on the dots. He had amazing sight. Years of trail-craft and constant danger had endowed him with razor-sharp perceptions.

The dark shapes were not slinking coyotes. They were undoubtedly horsemen. They were riding at a walk across the desert, and their direction would take them past the posse's hideout.

The riders could be only Krafton Webber and his outfit. No one else would be heading this way at night.

There was no danger so far. But this was proof that Webber was still on their trail. It raised one question:

Why?

The thought brought back Jed's previous ideas about the outlaw not knowing that Andrew Platt had stopped a slug.

Jed was sure Webber would not trail back just to start another shooting parley. Webber had plenty to lose in such an action. It seemed that Krafton Webber was tracking back to the border in a search for the Texan posse, and there could be only one reason. Webber thought Andrew Platt was still alive, and he wanted him because he was a sure-fire guide to the bonanza.

But, thought Jed grimly, the old fellow was sure dead. He was dead and buried. He would not act as guide to anyone.

Jed stayed motionless as the distant night riders went on into the darkness and were lost.

Jed Ryland stayed alert on the top of the crag for a long time. He thought that Krafton Webber might turn on the trail and ride round until he located the Texan posse-men.

But, in the dim moonlight, Webber and his owl-hoots had evidently lost the trail. They thought they could overtake Ezra Strang's men by riding on in the direction of Monument City. They had not realised that the posse had ridden off the direct trail and made camp in a hideout basin.

While Jed Ryland was keeping alert, Texas Callahan and Webber were riding side by side. The tired animals plodded on. The men knew it was impossible to rowel any speed into them. Being wise to horses and their ways, they did not attempt to spur them on to a crippled condition.

"Blastit!" snarled Krafton Webber for the hundredth time. "Those durned rannigans must be ridin' on all night!"

Texas Callahan hunched in the saddle. Despite his deceptively slovenly style of riding, he was ready to uncoil like a rattler.

"What happens ef those ginks git back to Monument?" he asked. "They'll hole-up in the town and all hell won't git 'em out. They'll guard Andrew Platt night an' day."

"We'll trail up to 'em afore they hit town!" snarled Webber.

The slow ride went on. The horses were obviously trail weary. There had been a great deal of riding all day.

They rode into the maze of outcrops that marked the end of the desert plains. They were near the border. They were still some twenty miles from Monument City.

Then one of the border breeds, pushing his horse around a clump of prickly pear growing out of jagged rocks, felt the animal go lame. For a few yards the cayuse hobbled on, and then the breed called to Krafton Webber.

"Amigo, my hoss is kinda lame. What now?"

"Durn yuh hoss!" snarled Webber.

The party halted to consider. The outlaws totalled only six now that Chub Negler was gone. Krafton Webber did not want to lose any more men. Maybe after the gold was found, he would not care a hoot if the rannigans died. But right now men meant guns. He could let the man bed down somewhere while the rest pushed on. The man could be picked up later, or his horse might recover with rest.

"Ain't no good goin' on," snapped one of the men. He was a white ruffian with a gun rep. Webber knew him for a hard hombre. "The durned hosses need rest."

"Yuh want to git thet gold?" snapped Webber.

"Shore, we want gold!" retorted the man. "We want thet old buzzard's gold more'n anything. But I figger we got to rest these critters afore they all go lame on us. I figger a bit o' hard riding to-morrer will catch us up wi' those posse-men."

"He's right," growled Texas Callahan. "Anyways, I figger those hellions are holed-up somewhere in this blastit territory."

Webber considered.

"Mebbe yuh're right," he conceded. "An' we couldn't find those fellers in the night."

"We could walk into a dry-gulch," said Texas Callahan.

Krafton Webber made up his mind.

"All right. Git offen the hosses soon as yuh see some grass for the critters. We'll camp."

About half a mile further on they found a spot which was suitable. Grass grew in tufts between cholla cactus and mesquite bushes. There were sandy patches for the men to lie on. Some of the breeds just flopped down and rolled cigarettes. Not one had a fodder bag for the horses. They had made no preparations for the ride out.

Krafton Webber sat staring grimly into the wan moonlight.

"A helluva set-up!" he snarled to his side-kick. "I got half a map to a bonanza. Kin yuh remember what Platt said about finding an Injun trail atween twin peaks?"

"A bit. I was reckoning on a map—an' Andrew Platt to take us up thar."

"We'll git thet hombre yet!" vowed Webber.

He continued to think that Ezra Strang had rescued Andrew Platt from the cantina.

"We'll git thet old catamount supposin' we got to shoot a way right into Monument!" snarled Krafton Webber.

It was night in the desert. One of the horses was lame, and the others were plenty tired. There was nothing to do but bed down and get some rest.

"Soon as sun-up, we git goin'," rapped Webber, as boss. "Mebbe thet hoss will be stronger by sun-up, amigo."

The border breed nodded.

Ten minutes later the place was silent except for the odd movement of a horse as it nosed for grass.

The owl-hoots were hard characters, but they had no sense of discipline. Webber had thought of appointing a camp guard, but he knew quite well the man would just drop off to sleep. He could have done the job himself, or asked Texas Callahan, but he decided to chance the whole thing. In any case, Ezra Strang and his men were probably ahead or holed-up for the night in the same way.

For some time there was a complete silence over the camp. Men sprawled, heads on rough pillows of sand and hats. The night was still warm. The heat was still in the sand. There was no possibility of rain because it was not due to rain for another two months!

While the outlaws slept, ready in truth to leap up and claw for gun at the slightest sound, a rider approached the site. He dismounted from his horse about half a mile from the outlaw camp and ground-hitched the animal.

Then the man walked on slowly, yard by yard. His eyes were fixed on the spot where he had seen the outlaw riders halt. As he came nearer, creeping over the rocks, he saw that the men had made a camp, as he had surmised.

He came over the ground very patiently, watching. He saw the stretched-out forms and the horses.

He took out his guns.

Jose Petrillio never took chances with his oily skin. If he was taking chances now, it was because he was very interested in the other half of a map.

9

JED RYLAND wakened Ezra Strang. It did not take much doing. All he needed was to lay a hand on the sheriff's shoulder. The next instant Ezra was scooping for his Colt!

"Yuh kin put thet away!" chuckled Jed.

"What in tarnation d'yuh want? Want me to take over guard?"

"Nope. I've just spotted Webber's outfit."

Sheriff Strang sat bolt upright.

"Whar? Them hellions around hyar?"

"Nope. I figger they've ridden off a few miles. Now lissen, hombre. I want to go after them. I just wakened yuh to tell yuh thet."

"What yuh aim to do? Kill the varmints all by yoreself?"

"Nope. Shut up and lissen. I'm goin' to trail 'em and see if I kin surprise

225

Webber with a chance shot. Thet jigger's got the map to Platt's bonanza."

"Platt's bonanza." grunted Ezra Strang. "I guess it will go down in history as thet! So yuh figger to git the map offen Webber all by yoreself?"

"Mebbe. It's just an idee. Okay, I'm goin'. No need to waken the others."

"Mebbe we wouldn't ha' camped hyar if I'd figgered Webber was after us," grunted Ezra. "What in tarnation does he want to ride after us fer? Ain't he got the map?"

"I reckon he figgers Andrew Platt is still alive."

Ezra nearly laughed aloud.

"Shore he is—hell! Yep, he must figger the old coot is alive to come ridin' after us. Shore. I see it. He wants Andrew Platt as a guide."

"Yeah, that's it. Wal, I'm a-goin', podner."

"Hold it!" hissed Ezra Strang. "How come yuh figger yuh doing this alone?"

"It's my meat. I kin trail 'em. Mebbe

I won't git near enough. They might tumble to me pronto."

Ezra Strang got to his feet, grabbed at his saddle.

"I'm a-goin' with yuh! I'll tell Hank Carter we're a-goin'."

"Darn it, yuh'll have Hank Carter wantin' to go with me next!" snapped Jed.

"He won't. He's under orders. I say he stays hyar. This is just an Injun prowl anyways."

Hank Carter was aroused and told everything. Just as Jed had thought, he wanted to accompany them. But Ezra told him he had to keep a camp.

The way Jed Ryland saw it, there was just a bare chance of catching sight of Webber's outfit. He had wanted to scout ahead and then report back to Sheriff Strang, but Ezra had hog-tied that idea.

They would have to scout ahead together, and then report back to the other posse-men if there was any chance of bushwhacking Webber's band!

Ezra Strang soon had the cinch fastened

on his horse. A minute later he and Jed rode off, taking a trail through the bizarre abutments of rock which scored the land.

The cayuses had profited by a rest and were ready for a few miles.

Jed Ryland led the way, riding his horse expertly through the jumbled terrain. He had fastened his direction on the curve of land just ahead. He had last seen Webber's outfit ride out of sight around that ridge.

Some twenty minutes later, following a track through the outcrops, they almost blundered on the outlaw camp.

Jed grinned grimly when he realised that the two outfits had camped almost within two miles of each other. In the pale light and surrounded by jagged, rocky terrain they did not realise they were so near each other.

Jed and Ezra dismounted and ground-hitched the horses in a rocky basin from which they would not stray. Then, gun in hand, they crept forward, belly to the rocky tableland which edged up to the outlaw camp.

They had hardly got the sleeping forms of the owl-hoot men in focus again when they saw a mysterious figure steal up close to the sleeping men!

"Who'n heck's thet?" hissed Ezra. "D'yuh see thet?"

"Yeah. Some hombre stealin' up like an Injun."

Jed Ryland stared grimly through the wan light, scarcely crediting his eyes. But he had good eyes, he knew, and the man bending over a sleeping figure was operating with the silence of an Indian.

Jed and Ezra held their gunfire in the face of the mysterious actions going on. They watched, and although there were times when the figure bending over the prone man was blurred into darkness, they saw enough to puzzle them.

Then the man jumped up and ran for dear life. As he did so a gun barked after him. It was sheer luck that the running man slithered to a crevice at the same moment the six-gun exploded.

The next second guns were hacking redly at the night as outlaws wakened and triggered at any shadow they fancied moved.

The mysterious man had disappeared. Even Jed, from the angle of the higher ground, could not see the man. He had vanished in the rocky outcrops.

The first gunshots ceased to roar. The owl-hoots were taking stock of the situation. All at once a voice which Jed recognised as Texas Callahan's, bawled in rage.

"The skunk has slugged Webber! Go git thet rat, men!"

There were further cries, but Jed Ryland and Ezra Strang were interested only in the first bawl of fury.

"Slugged! What's thet mean?" whispered Jed.

"I figger thet hombre—whoever he was —rapped Webber on the head," said Ezra. "Now why in tarnation would a gink do thet?"

"You ask me an easy one," said Jed. "Who was the feller, anyways?"

They really did not know. The man was evidently not one of the outlaw mob.

And he was certainly not one of the Texan posse-men.

Jed Ryland's keen wits saw several angles, but they seemed too incredible. He stopped thinking because there was work to do.

"Give 'em a taste o' lead, podner!" he rapped.

Ezra had been waiting for Jed to come to some decision. As the outlaws in the camp below dispersed after the other running man, Jed and Ezra pumped lead at the targets.

The exploding Colts and the flashes of red attracted the return fire of the owl-hoots in less than a second.

Quite soon a regular rataplan of fire was barking from both sides.

In the shooting Texas Callahan made the mistake of thinking that the attackers were the ones who had slugged Krafton Webber. So he rallied the outlaws and shooting became concentrated on the red flashes coming from the ledge not far away.

As the outlaws fired at Jed and Ezra, a

burly gentleman in a store suit, the trousers of which were tucked into riding boots, was making all haste to a horse less than half a mile away.

Jose Petrillio was a bit unhappy about the shooting, but not one slug came his way. He thought that a bit queer. Once he looked back and saw red gun flashes stabbing from opposite sides. He thought two parties were having a shindig.

Suddenly he realised that the Texan posse-men had arrived and were shooting at Webber's gun-hawks. That could be the only explanation.

Jose Petrillio stumbled and ran through the gullies and reached his horse. He was almost devoid of breath. Running at full speed was not his usual habit. He much preferred the cunning move.

Well, he figured he had made a cunning move. Hastily stuffed into his pocket was the second half of the bonanza map.

He had taken it out of Krafton Webber's shirt pocket. He had worked softly. He had been able to administer a deft blow to Webber's head which had stopped the outlaw boss from moving even as he had realised he was being attacked.

Jose Petrillio had had time to unbutton the shirt pocket and fumble for the paper. He had been lucky in getting it quickly. For one of the breed outlaws had sensed movement and danger.

As the man had sat up, Jose had ran out—with the sheet of paper.

The breed had fired rather wildly. And Jose Petrillio had slid to a crack in the rocks which was a natural passage to safety.

Jose Petrillio jumped to the saddle of the ground-hitched horse and applied Mexican spurs.

The animal sprang away, guided to the flat terrain and headed for the distant El Grande.

Sheriff Jose Petrillio had tracked Webber patiently and succeeded in his aim.

Back at the shooting foray, Jed Ryland figured the lead swapping might go on all night. For one thing, it was dark and the moon was not enough to give good visibility. Most of the time they were firing at red gun-flashes. The outlaws were holed-up behind rocks.

After trying a few shots, in the hope that they would get one of the owl-hoots, Jed Ryland thought he sensed a movement on the part of the other gun-slingers.

Red flashes and exploding guns were appearing from another side of them. Slugs whined furiously, close enough to send up rock chips in their faces. They had to keep low behind the rock they had selected.

"Those jiggers are tryin' to take us from another side!" he hissed.

"Yuh tellin' me!" snapped Ezra Strang, ducking as an angry slug whined overhead.

"Let's git out o' hyar!" decided Jed.

It was wise thought. They were only two against many. They could be undoubtedly surrounded. There was not a rock made that could give cover on all four sides.

They gradually drew back until they were out of Colt range. They stopped their own shooting because they did not want to give away their movements. Very soon they reached the horses. They hit the saddles and urged the mounts back in the direction of the posse camp. Within a minute the rocky outcrops gave them enough cover to stop a Gatling gun.

The shooting ceased when Webber's cohorts realised there was no return fire.

Jed and Ezra rode into the Texan camp and found the men on the alert. They had heard the distant shooting. Hank Carter had told them all he knew.

Jed and Ezra gave the latest news. The information about the mysterious man who had got away from both parties caused much speculation.

"So Webber got slugged?" mused Jed Ryland. "Shore is a pity the hombre didn't finish him. Who would want to Injun up and slug Webber?"

"Plenty o' ginks, I guess," muttered Ezra.

"Yep. Mebbe. But how many would really do it? And why?"

"I warn't no good at problems in the schoolhouse," grumbled Ezra Strang.

"Neither was I, podner. Wal, what now?"

"We got to light out," said Ezra. "Ain't no good camping close to an enemy. I shore know the answer to thet one, amigo!"

The sheriff of Monument City was perfectly right. They had to get right away or ambush might come to them.

Horses were saddled and the party began to ride again. There was no safety in a camp with Webber's gunhawks around. Attack under night conditions was not a good prospect, either. Ezra Strang, as leader of the posse, decided it was better to move and figure out plans in the light of day.

The ride went on all night, slowly and laboriously at times. When the pale light of dawn came they were past Webber's one-time hideout in the hills, and the valley was just ahead. Ten miles up the valley lay Monument City.

They rode into town with the first flush of sun-up. The sun was visible in the east, climbing to another hot day.

Jed rode to Ezra Strang's home behind his sheriff's office. There was nowhere else for him to stay. Ezra asked him in. Jed clumped in stiffly.

"Gosh, I'm shore trail weary! Wal, I figger to git spruced up."

The remainder of the posse-men had dispersed to their homes. They spread the word that Andrew Platt was dead, killed during a gun-fight. The people of the town had seen the men ride in. Soon the news was all over the place. Folks were just getting astir for the morning.

Jed Ryland was grim and tight-faced. It was not just lack of sleep which tightened his nerves. He was thinking grimly all the time about the map. Krafton Webber had a map. The man certainly could not ride to the Guadalupes without preparation. The ride itself would take a few days. Finding the bonanza might even take longer even with a map.

Jed Ryland had seen Andrew Platt draw the map under threat of terrible torture, and he did not think that the map was a fake. Andrew Platt had been all in when he made a plan of the location of his gold mine.

Jed Ryland spruced himself up and borrowed a new black-and-white check gabardine shirt from Ezra. He sent a young lad—who had arrived to see if there was work for him—to the stores with money and instructions to get new clothes. Jed wanted a hat, and he did not care what colour it was as long as it was his size. He gave the youngster instructions about new pants.

"Ain't yuh goin' to git some shut-eye?" asked Ezra.

"Nope. I aim to pay a visit."

"When yuh figger to set off for the Guadalupes, let me know," commented Ezra grimly. "The news will git around thet Andrew Platt is dead. I allus figgered thet Webber had some rannigans in this town in his pay. It wouldn't surprise me ef Webber soon gits a contact an' hears thet Platt is dead."

"I wonder whar Webber an' his outfit are now," mused Jed. "I figger Webber was after us because he thought Andrew Platt was with us alive. But when he learns thet the old gink is plumb dead, he'll change his plans."

The boy arrived with the new gear. Jed was spruced up when he got into the new clothes. Jed had washed dust and blood from his head. There was just a bruise where the shale had slugged him.

Jed Ryland got into the tight-fitting brown pants which were the fashion of the day. He had the check shirt over broad shoulders. He fastened a new yellow bandanna around his neck. The boy had brought a good fawn Stetson which had cost plenty. Jed had polished his riding boots until they shone a bright black again. His gun-belts had had a good cleaning, too. The holster of one was empty. When Webber had trapped Ezra and himself in the Santa Alicia room, the outlaw had taken their guns. Jed had gotten a gun from the dead Chub Negler. He did not like the gun. He intended to go out and buy new Colts at one of the town's gun emporiums. He only wished he could get his roan back from Texas Callahan—but that might be achieved some day, he thought.

"Yuh figger to go some place all dressed up like a fancy pants?" demanded Ezra.

"Yep. I'm goin' to see someone."

"Who the heck is thet? Yuh goin' to git measured for a burial casket?"

And Ezra Strang chuckled at his own rough joke.

Jed slapped his back.

"Nope, durn yuh! I'm a-goin' to see a gal name o' Jean Marsh. She's got a caravan in town, ain't she? Should be easy to find in this burg."

"What for yuh want to see a gal?"

"I jest said I'd see her when I got back," snapped Jed. "Maybe I got to account fer all my actions to an old coot like yuh? She's just lost her paw, ain't she? She'll be interested to hear about Webber, I guess."

"Quit making excuses," grunted Ezra. "I figger yuh want to see the gal because she's—wal, jest a gal!"

"Have it yore way," retorted Jed Ryland. "Anyways, soon as I git me some new hoglegs, I'm thinking of riding out for sign o' Krafton Webber. Thet map rightfully belongs to Andrew Platt, dead or alive. I got a mission to hang or kill Webber and his cohorts. I figger Webber is either jest outside this town or headin' fer the Guadalupes or making preparations back in El Grande. I ain't done with thet border hellion!"

And Jed went out on that, grim but smiling serenely.

He stopped at a gun emporium and tried some of the new six-guns. He got two which seemed good to his hands. He paid for them with the money he carried in his belt. He strode on through the town, feeling better with the Colts lying heavily in the holsters. He was wearing his Texas Ranger silver badge, and also Ezra Strang's deputy badge.

He was conscious of a few keen glances as he made his way down the dusty stem. Buckboards were clattering into town with ranchers from the outlying spreads coming in to buy stores. Already the saloons had their quota of customers. The barber, the blacksmith and the school-marms were busy. Down at the stock-yards, cattlemen argued prices with buyers. At the stage and freight depot a Concord coach was drawn up ready for the trip to Laredo. With sun-up Monument City was sure getting into its stride. There was plenty of lawlessness in Monument City, but the town had other business besides killing.

Jed Ryland found Jean Marsh at her four-wheeled caravan. She was making up ointments and putting them into boxes. The two horses were evidently in some livery. Jed guessed the girl had found the caravan intact when she had got away from Webber's hideout, and she had driven the outfit into town herself. Then she had got into Webber's way again when the outlaws surprised her leaving Andrew Platt's home. But that was all over now.

"Howdy, Miss," called Jed softly.

She was sitting on the steps. She was wearing a gingham dress, and her red hair was long and wavy.

As he spoke she looked up quickly.

"Oh, you're back! I'm glad! Tell me what happened?"

"Andrew Platt's dead," he said grimly. "The sheriff rode back because he figgered nuthin' more could be done. But Webber has a plan showing the location of the bonanza."

And he told her all about it.

"I'm a-goin' back after thet hombre an' his outfit," he concluded grimly. "I've got instructions from headquarters to stick hyar as long as necessary."

"I'm glad you came to see me," she breathed.

"Yuh stayin' in town long?" he asked.

"I'm thinking of selling the caravan and

243

the contents. I'm not a doctor, you know."

As she began to laugh, he joined in.

"Mebbe I ought to git me some ointment!" he joked. "I might need it afore long!"

"You'll have to be careful!" she said.

"I'll be careful," he returned gravely.

Hastily, with a red spot in each cheek, she changed the subject.

"If I sell the caravan, I might stay here and teach. I've been told I can get a job teaching in the school."

"It's a mighty fine little city!" he pronounced. "Not as big as San Antonio, where I hail from, but still a mighty fine little town. When Krafton Webber is finished, mebbe the folks round hyar will git some peace. Thet hombre used to raid banks and stages."

"When are you goin' after that outlaw?" she asked.

He smiled gravely. Light danced in his blue eyes and light reflected in his straw-coloured hair as he held his hat in hand.

"I aim to git goin' right now. I jest

want a fresh hoss and mebbe a rifle and a saddle-bag with grub. I'll cross sign o' thet feller pretty quick. If he aims to take his outfit to the Guadalupes, there's a fair amount o' time."

And with that he had to leave her. He did so awkwardly because he had made an amazing discovery. He had found out why he wanted to talk to Jean Marsh. He wanted to talk to her because—well— goldarn it—she was the finest girl he had ever seen!

As he walked away he figured he would soon be back to Monument City. There was plenty to come back for!

He was busy at the livery behind Ezra's office. He got the ostler saddle a big strong bay. He did not intend to buy a rifle when he could borrow one with plenty of ammunition from Ezra Strang. He also made up a grubstake from the sheriff's stocks. Ezra Strang watched this with grim interest.

"Ain't yuh goin' to rest?"

"Nope. I kin rest in the saddle. I figger

to meet up with Webber. He's got no right to thet map."

"Whar d'yuh think he'll be?"

"Wal, he'll soon learn thet Andrew Platt's dead. He won't be coming to Monument City in thet case. He'll be back in El Grande gittin' ready for the ride to the Guadalupes."

"I got the idee he didn't ride after us last night," muttered Ezra.

"Mebbe he turned back on the trail. Thet's what I figger."

Ezra Strang looked grimly out of a window. He was not seeing anything in particular.

"I'm ridin' with yuh, amigo. Shore, I know we cayn't do anything for Andrew Platt now. He's dead—mighty dead. But thet map don't belong to Webber. I cayn't ask a posse to ride into thet durned Guadalupe wilderness. These men have jobs and businesses to attend to. It was all right when Andrew Platt was alive. Thet was somethin to ride for. Nope, I'm a-comin' with yuh, hombre."

"Yuh're the sheriff hyar. Mebbe the townsfolk won't like it."

"I kin do what I like!" roared Ezra. "Webber's an outlaw, ain't he?"

"He's in Mexico now," Jed pointed out gravely.

"Don't make no difference. He's wanted fer crimes in this town!" bawled the sheriff. "I kin appoint a deputy to keep things runnin' while I'm a-ridin' with yuh! All right! I don't want any more argufying! We're ridin' after thet durned owl-hoot!"

10

KRAFTON WEBBER rode side by side with Texas Callahan, and the other outlaws jigged horses along behind. Webber was cursing the futile night ride. His shoulder ached plenty. But most of all he was cursing one Jose Petrillio.

"Thet oily snakeroo! Thet slinkin' greaser! I knew him! I got my lamps on him! Bending over me ... then the coyote slugged me ..."

Texas stared ahead at the huddle of shacks and adobe huts that marked the outskirts of El Grande. With the morning sun, heat hazes were beginning to dance over the desert again.

"Wal, he got thet part o' the map," said Texas Callahan. "How the hell d'yuh figger he knew we had a map?"

"He's an oily snake," snapped Webber. "Thet's enough. He trailed us, crept up on me like a dirty Injun. He knew durned fine what he was after. I saw his dirty pan afore he slugged me! Wal, I'll blast his guts when I sight him! I'll git thet map back."

"We've still got to git the other half from Andrew Platt," Texas Callahan rapped. His black, half-breed eyes were snapping with rage. He was figuring Webber was slipping. Maybe a hombre could do better without Krafton Webber . . .

The outlaw boss ground strong, yellowed teeth together.

"Hell's bells! We ain't gittin' nowhere. Ezra Strang has thet old desert rat back in Monument City with the half-map. And Jose Petrillio has the other half! Wal, I figger we kin deal pretty quick with Jose! Then we make a gun-play fer Platt and the other half. Ain't no other way to do it!"

"Shore as hell we're startin' all over again!" grumbled Texas Callahan.

The other members of the owl-hoot band had been grousing in undertones on the ride back to El Grande. They knew the truth. The torn half of the map had been filched from Krafton Webber by Jose Petrillio. In their eyes Webber had lost some prestige.

Krafton Webber knew this. He was leader of the outfit simply by impressing the other with his power and brains. The only thing keeping them together was the thought of gold. Before that, when on the stage and bank raids, it had been the easy profits. Webber had been clever and lucky—a good combination. Right now, his luck seemed to be running out.

The outfit rode weary horses into El Grande. They did not go right up to the Santa Alicia. They figured they might run into trouble.

They stopped at the first cantina they reached. They led the horses into a livery and told the Mexican wrangler to clean them down and feed and water the critters.

Then Webber and Texas Callahan, leading the men, rolled into the saloon, feet clumping tiredly against the sand-strewn boards. They ordered red-eye and threw it down as if it was water.

The fight with Jed and Ezra Strang in the rocky country had reduced the rannigans under Webber's command to four, not including Texas. Krafton Webber figured this was plenty to share the gold —if and when they found it. He did not care about the dead hombres he had left on the trail. They had lived by the gun and died in cold fire.

The drink restored the outlaws' energy. They were hungry, but that could wait. With several drinks inside them, they felt savagely prepared for anything. Tiredness evaporated. They felt good, even though they were outwardly dusty, sweat-streaked men with whisker stubble black on their faces.

"Aw right!" snarled Webber. "Let's go git thet snake, Jose Petrillio. I ain't planning anything. Ef he don't hand over thet half map, I'll blast him!"

Full of anger and drink, the six men lurched down the road. They seemed to walk clumsily, but it was the combined effect of high-heel boots in the rough street, tiredness and the drink. They were grimly dangerous men and would dive for hardware at a moment's notice.

But first they had to locate Jose Petrillio and learn about the half map.

The obvious place was the Santa Alicia saloon. They thrust roughly through the batwing doors and stared around. Webber grabbed the shoulder of a half-breed server who was walking to a table.

"Whar's Jose Petrillio?"

The man rolled his eyes to the top of the stairs. Webber glared up to the balcony.

"Up thar, is he? Talk, yuh rat!"

"Señor, Petrillio may be in his room!" stuttered the man.

Krafton Webber flung him away. The server went back fully five yards and crashed against a table. Two vaqueros at the table half-rose, but they did not go for guns. The savage expressions on the outlaws' faces deterred them.

Six men stamped across the cantina floor, eyes warily watching for gun-play.

They reached the stairs and began to climb. The vaqueros sat down slowly. Trouble might be coming to Jose Petrillio, but that was nothing to them.

In a minute the six rannigans strode down the passage which led to Jose Petrillio's private room. Webber knew the door.

He did not bother to knock.

He motioned to Texas Callahan to work his trick. Webber could not pull it because his shoulder was still sore.

Texas Callahan rammed all his great weight and strength against the door. Stout it was, but the lock gave with a crack. Wood splintered and the door slammed inwards. The six men plunged in, guns drawn.

They halted inside the room and slowly moved fanwise.

Jose Petrillio maintained a greasy smile. His hands were well away from his gun-butts.

"Howdy, amigos! You sure make the noise when you enter my room!"

"Cut out the yap!" snarled Webber.

"We want the map yuh took from me! Give!"

But Jose Petrillio continued to smile, and seeing it Krafton Webber realised he was up against a tricky hombre. Maybe gun-slinging would not get the answers.

"Please put your guns away, señors. We will talk like caballeros. You want that half of a map?"

"Shore. Whar is it?" snapped Webber.

"It is hidden, my friend. And if you shoot me you will never know where to look. Now we talk business, huh?"

Very slowly Krafton Webber put his guns back in his holsters and sat down in a chair. His big red face turned sombrely to Sheriff Jose Petrillio.

"What's on your mind?"

Jose Petrillio slipped fingers into a box on the table and brought out a thin black cigar. He shoved the box over to Krafton Webber.

"Where is the other half of the map?" asked Jose Petrillio calmly.

Krafton Webber stared.

"All right, amigo," he sneered. "I'll

254

play alawng with yuh. But don't complain if yuh git hurt somewheres! Yuh want to know about the other half o' the map? Wal, thet old jigger we had in this saloon was taken away last night by those Texan posse-men an' thet old buzzard had the other half o' the map. I figger he snatched it when the shootin' started. I didn't know thet at the time. But it's the only answer. So yuh want to know who has the other half o' the map? Wal, it's thet old desert rat, Andrew Platt o' Monument City."

Jose Petrillio continued to smile greasily. His smile did not expand or contract. It did not alter.

He was thinking. And he certainly did not reveal that he had any secrets to the assembled outlaws.

Jose Petrillio did not know much about Andrew Platt beyond a few rumours which had been brought into El Grande by drifters from Monument City.

Jose Petrillio did not really care what had happened to Andrew Platt. If the Texans had taken him back to his home, it was not so important. Because Jose knew darned well that he had both halves of the bonanza map.

He had been studying it, and knew full well the significance of the complete plan.

"So this Andrew Platt hombre has one half of the map and I have the other half, señors," murmured Jose.

Webber breathed menacingly: "Yeah!"

"That is what you call too bad," continued Jose Petrillio. "For you, amigos, have nothing!"

Texas Callahan produced his gun impatiently.

"Hand over durn yuh! I ain't one fer all this blamed yap!"

Webber snarled to him: "Take it easy!"

"That is right, amigo," said Jose Petrillio soothingly. "Take it easy like your friend. Remember, we are doing business."

"All right, you've got the half map," snapped Webber. "What do yuh figger? Yuh got a proposition?"

Jose Petrillio nodded, and struck a match and applied it to his cigar.

"It is simple. I am your partner. I am the partner of all you mens. I will keep the little bit of map in case you figure to kill your partner. In the meantime, you look for the other half. Is that okay, señors?"

Krafton Webber breathed hard. He realised he was being played as smartly as he had played other men in the past.

The trouble was he just had no idea as yet how smartly he was being played!

"Yuh got the torn map hidden away?" he questioned hoarsely.

"Yes, amigo."

"Maybe yuh kin tell me. We ought to know if we're podners."

"When you get the other half, amigo, we will work together. We shall have to if we want to find the gold. We shall both have half a map."

"Maybe we could find the part o' the map yuh have if we searched this room," suggested Webber.

Jose Petrillio shook his head and sweat dropped on to the table.

"No, señors. My part of the map is

better hidden than that. And if I die, no ones will know where to look. The gold will still be the secret of this Platt hombre."

Krafton Webber came to a decision. He had to make up his mind and show some mastery to keep his leadership.

"All right, Jose. Yuh hang on to thet bit o' map. We're podners. Anyway, we got to git the other half afore the durned thing is any good. Maybe we'll git hold o' Andrew Platt again."

"Ef thet's happens, we won't need this coyote!" snarled one of the outlaws. "An' I'll ride back an' blast this ornery cuss, fer shore!"

Krafton Webber grinned unpleasantly at Jose Petrillio's momentary anxiety.

"See, hombre? Guess there's a few angles to this deal as yet."

His smile a trifle grim, Jose Petrillio reflected that there were many angles, as the other called them. One of the angles was that he had the complete map!

"If you get this old man to show you

to the gold, I have lost, señors," he said placatingly.

He reflected that it did not matter what he said as long as he kept his secret. For his intention was to organise an expedition into the Guadalupes with, perhaps, a trusted companion. While Webber was trying to get a portion of map from a man who did not possess it, he, Jose Petrillio, would be busy.

Krafton Webber stood up, held his shoulder as a bit of pain throbbed momentarily.

"All right, keep thet bit of map in case we don't git Andrew Platt again. Half a map is no good to yuh, hombre!"

With the decision, the men walked grudgingly out of the room, leaving Jose staring.

"I figgered we rode back hyar to git thet map!" said Texas Callahan violently.

"He's got a damned good bluff, ain't he? Mebbe yuh would kill him? Then what? It jest wouldn't do any good. We got plenty o' time to blast thet greasy snake."

259

"Goldarn it, I suppose we got to ride back to Monument City again," grumbled Texas. "I'm shore tired o' hittin' thet trail!"

As they walked down to the saloon and had another drink, the general conclusion was that it would be better to concentrate on getting Andrew Platt again. If they achieved that, they would gain the whip hand again.

Webber little guessed that was an impossible feat!

He spent some time drinking and resting. He thought all around the problem. Jose had played a check card. But if Andrew Platt destroyed his half of the map, Jose Petrillio would have a joker as his only trump.

An hour later, after Krafton Webber had got medical attention from a renegade "doctor" in the town the men went along for their horses.

They found they were still a long way from fresh. So Webber made a trade for six new animals, with a cash adjustment. Grudgingly, he parted with the dollar

260

bills. He would just as easily have paid the liveryman with a slug, but he thought maybe they might need the man's help again.

Jed Ryland's roan, which he thought a great deal about, was thus left in the Mexican livery. With new animals, the band set out. They passed a gunsmith store and stopped to buy more cold ammunition. Rifles were in saddle-boots and they had bullets for them in plenty. A bit further on in the stinking township, they got grub from another store. Once again Webber parted with greenbacks in exchange for salted bacon, beans, coffee and flour.

Then they cantered the horses out towards the border.

"Hell, we're shore burning up this trail!" sneered Texas Callahan to the man he was riding beside. The man was a white rannigan. He was the hard customer who had contradicted Webber many times before. His name was Rork Doonan, and he had had good Irish parents, but he did not take after them.

"Yep, an' mebbe we're no nearer to thet gold!" muttered the man.

With Chub Negler dead, Texas Callahan was inclined to link up with the man as a side-kick.

"Aw, hell, we jest got bad luck!" snapped another man.

They rode on through the heat of the day and found themselves near the border and among the broken, volcanic rock-land which rose from the desert bed.

It was Texas Callahan's keen black eyes which sighted the signs which spelled a one-time camp to him. He saw horse droppings and scooped up sand which had served as beds. There were imprints of horses' hoofs. But there had not been a fire. The remains of the camp were surrounded by rocky boulders which made a sort of barricade.

"Say, thet ain't the camp we had last night, though it's pretty near, at thet!"

Krafton Webber swung around in the saddle.

"Must ha' bin those posse-men. Shore,

thet's whar the hellions camped—not a durned mile or two from us."

Standing in the stirrups, with his horse reined to a halt, Texas looked over the spot with interest.

"What the heck's thet heap o' rocks over thar?"

Curiously, he jigged his horse closer, into the basin. Not far from where men had lain and horses had been tethered, he found a rough cairn of rocks.

"One o' those rannigans stopped a slug!" he rapped to Webber. "Thar's a gink buried hyar. Wonder who it kin be?"

With a sudden vault Krafton Webber got down from his cayuse and led it over to the spot.

As he met up with Texas Callahan and stared at the cairn, he got a powerful hunch. It was, however, based on swift thinking. He saw a way to strengthen his leadership among the owl-hoots.

"Git those durned stones offen thet grave," he ordered.

"Heck of a lot o' rocks!" muttered

Rork Doonan. "What difference does it make who's lyin' hyar?"

Krafton Webber snarled triumphantly: "Yuh figger yuh got brains, huh? Wal, let me tell yuh I got to think for the whole passel o' yuh. Yuh wanted to blast Jose Petrillio. Git the rocks offen this one-man boothill an' we'll see iffen that was a smart idee!"

"What's on yore mind?" asked Texas Callahan.

"Jest this!" grated Webber. "There was only three jiggers in thet room at the Santa Alicia when the shootin' started— Ezra Strang, Jed Ryland and Andrew Platt. We didn't kill any o' thet posse, and I'm blamed shore they weren't nicked, judgin' by the way they lighted out. If a gink had been badly hit, he'd ha' dropped or slowed the others. Nope, they got to the hosses and rode away. I got a hunch if anyone was killed, it was one o' them three in the room."

"But I'm durned shore it was Jed Ryland and Ezra Strang throwing lead at us jest after Jose Petrillio got away last night!" Texas Callahan halted his words suddenly and then swung to the cairn of rocks. "Say, what if it's Andrew Platt?"

"See yuh're usin' yore head," sneered Webber. "Go git them rocks off thet heap. Mebbe I'm wrong. I shore hope so!"

But five minutes later they were staring at the corpse of Andrew Platt as it lay in the sandy crevice.

"Dead!" rasped Krafton Webber. "Wal, ain't that dandy!"

"The map! Who yuh figger has the map half now?" asked Texas swiftly.

"Thet hellion Jed Ryland—or Ezra Strang!" choked Webber. "Who else?"

"Yeah. They'd git the half when they got Andrew Platt out o' thet room," Texas hammered out.

Krafton Webber rammed a horned hand against his thigh.

"Ef those fools destroy thet half o' the map, we're roped and thrown!" he rasped.

There was a definite silence while the

men digested this viewpoint. It was not a pleasant thought.

"Yuh mean the bonanza is lost if thet part o' the map is torned up?" grated Rork Doonan.

"What else?" sneered Webber. "Yuh figger yuh could find the gold with half a map?"

"They won't tear thet half up!" panted Texas Callahan. "Hell, no! Mebbe them hombres are jest as interested in the gold as any other jiggers! And I figger they got to report to the State authorities. Thet gink, Jed Ryland, got to report to his captin, ain't he? They won't tear thet part o' the map up."

"Maybe yuh're right," retorted Webber. "I shore hope thet's right. So Jose Petrillio has one half and Jed Ryland or Ezra Strang the other half."

Texas Callahan threw himself to the saddle, jigged his horse away from the basin.

"Ain't no use lookin' fer Andrew Platt now!" he yelled. "Guess we've got to git thet map offen those two hombres an' then make a deal with Jose!"

The whole party got back to leather and jigged away from the spot.

They had hardly got more than a hundred feet from the one-time camp when a rifle cracked across the silence of the wasteland.

The bullet sliced under Webber's arm as he held the reins in fine style.

The steel-jacketed shell dug fatally at the half-breed rannigan riding only inches from Webber.

The man gave a gasp and pitched from the saddle.

The next moment the owl-hoots were leaping for cover. As they ran in grim surprise, more bullets whanged near them.

But the shots missed the running men. In seconds, Webber's outfit were holed-up behind rocks. The horses ran in all directions.

Only one man splayed on the patch of shale and sand.

"Danged bushwhack!" gritted Krafton Webber.

"Ef I miss my guess, thet's Jed Ryland's shooting!" cried Texas Callahan savagely.

The outlaws located the direction of the shooting. They soon realised, by the sound of the shots, that only two men were using Winchesters. An expert could always judge how many men were firing from a given direction.

Down the glaring yellow trail, by an upsurge of rocky buttes towering a hundred feet, they saw the puffs of smoke which denoted the attackers.

"Them hellions must ha' seen us pretty quick," snapped Krafton Webber.

He hugged his Colt in his hand. He could shoot with only one hand because the recoil was not pleasant to his wounded shoulder.

Texas Callahan cursed. Not one of the owl-hoots had had time to get the rifles out of the saddle-holsters. The rifles were still with the horses. And the horses were out of reach unless a man cared to risk his hide.

"What the blazes are those fellers ridin' over the border for?" rapped Krafton Webber.

He was flat against a rock which was near to Texas Callahan.

"They aim to hound us down, I reckon," snapped the other.

"Shore, thet's what thet Ryland rannigan has set out to do. Must be after my hide, cuss him. Cayn't be after the other bit o' map. Maybe he figgers I've got it, though."

"All they got to do is tear the other half to bits," cursed Texas. "an' then the whole blamed thing is finished. They know Andrew Platt is buzzard bait."

Krafton Webber nodded. His grim eyes were on the terrain ahead. He wondered how they would get out of this trap. It was a trap because the two rannigans ahead had rifles and there were only Colts against them!

He went over the facts and theories again.

269

"They shore wouldn't ride jest to git the other half o' the map. All they got to do is destroy the durned half they've got an' then thet bonanza will stay a secret for hell knows how long."

"Shore aim to make us dead cusses!" snarled Texas. "Thet's all. A danged round-up!"

"I don't get it," muttered Webber. "How do Ezra Strang an' Jed Ryland figger to round up us lot?"

"Jest two ornery galoots," retorted Texas Callahan. "They can't take us in. Ain't this Mexico?"

"Shore, this is Mexico," rapped back Webber. "An' that's why I don't get it. Ezra Strang knows durned fine he ain't got the authority to come shootin' an' bustin' over hyar!"

"Wal, the hellion's doing it!"

As if in proof of this assertion, a burst of rifle-fire whined around them. Five outlaws hugged red rocks. The horses were spooked afresh and galloped further away from the exploding guns.

And then Krafton Webber realised that

the attackers were changing locations. The two men had moved to different shooting positions.

"Tryin' to git around us!" gritted the outlaw boss. "Hell, I wish I had my rifle!"

But in their haste to get to cover, the outlaws had left the Winchesters in the saddle-holsters.

After some minutes, during which the two law-men got closer, Krafton Webber heard Jed Ryland's voice raised to issue instructions.

"Come out with yore hands up, Webber."

"Yuh ain't got us yet!" roared the outlaw.

"We got rifles, feller. Come on out an' hand over thet map."

"Mebbe yuh want to git the gold yore-self!" bawled Webber.

"All we want is for yuh to give up fer a fair trial," rammed back Jed's voice. "Yuh got no right to thet map."

"We ain't a-comin' out!" thundered

Webber, the fury of his voice making his big red cheeks tremble.

"We'll come an git yuh with smoke-poles!" threatened the other sternly.

"Yuh got half o' thet map," roared Webber. "Figure it out for yoreself! We know Andrew Platt is dead! I tell yuh a deal, Mister Ryland. Me an' my podners got the other half of the map. Play up with us, Ryland, an' we kin find the bonanza and make a split. Stop shootin' and let's make a parley. Yuh got half o' the map, an' we got the other. Howsabout it, huh?"

Krafton Webber's words echoed over the rough jagged land. There was some silence from the big red bluffs. Then Jed Ryland's voice jagged out grimly.

"Yuh're tryin' some fool game, Webber. Yuh know durned fine we ain't got no part o' the map. Yuh got the blamed map, an' we figger to take it from yuh. Yuh'll be dead, Webber. Are yuh comin' out with yore hands up?"

Behind the red rock Krafton Webber

272

spat dust from his mouth and stared over to Texas Callahan.

"What the blazes are they talkin' about? Thet hombre's tryin' to fool me. Shore as snakes he's got half o' the map. Wasn't it torn outa my hand by thet danged cuss, Andrew Platt? What sort o' play is this? Ryland's shore to have thet half."

But thoughts were stirring in Texas Callahan's brain. He narrowed his black eyes.

"Play thet gink up, Webber. I shore wouldn't like to think that the map has been lost."

The idea struck Webber all at once. A savage, desperate expression etched deeply into his weatherbeaten face.

"Let's quit foolin', Ryland!" he roared. "We got only half the map. We were ridin' the trail back to Monument to git the other half offen yuh. Now play dice with me! Ain't yuh got thet map half?"

"We ain't got any o' the map!"

"Lissen, hombre, Andrew Platt tore half out o' my hand during the shindig!"

shouted Webber. "Don't fool me, damn yuh! Yuh must ha' got the other half offen Platt!"

"Andrew Platt was dead when we got him out o' the Santa Alicia," came Jed Ryland's stern voice. "We didn't git any map. The last I saw o' the map was yuh holdin' it in yore hand, Webber. Yuh aimin' to tell me yuh only got half?"

Krafton Webber exchanged grim glances with Texas Callahan.

"Go ahead," muttered Texas. "Won't do any harm to tell those hellions we ain't got the whole map."

Krafton Webber began to shout his answers.

"All we got is half the map. Ef yuh figger to git the map out o' us, yuh got yore loop tangled, Ryland!"

Krafton Webber realised the whole thing was tangled. As a matter of fact, he did not even possess half the map. Jose Petrillio had half . . .

The thought struck Webber like a blow in the face. Jose Petrillio!

It was an amazing idea, but an insistent

one. Jose Petrillio undoubtedly had one half of the torn map. Secondly, Jed Ryland and Ezra Strang apparently knew nothing about the bonanza map being torn. So the second half had to be somewhere. It was possible that it was lost. It might have been dropped to the ground.

A bleak expression crowded into Webber's eyes. He suddenly saw that the explanation of the mystery lay back in El Grande and certainly not with Jed Ryland. He had a strong hunch that Jose Petrillio was playing a cunning game.

"We're not interested in the map so much as yuh, Webber!" thundered Jed Ryland. "Don't matter if yuh lost half o' the map. Shore figger yuh won't find the gold now, Webber. We mean to take yuh back to Monument City. Are yuh a-comin' out with yore hands over yore head?"

"Yuh ain't got the drop on us, Ryland!" roared Webber. "We kin sit yar till hell freezes. An' don't be too shore we can't find the whole map!"

A rifle-shot whanged over Webber's

head close enough to fan the air near his face. Webber cursed and flattened down again behind the rock.

"Wal, ain't thet sweet!" swore Texas Callahan. "Ryland ain't got part o' the map, an' we ain't got part, either. Jose Petrillio got half. Whar in tarnation's the other half gotten?"

"We'll git out o' this," retorted Webber, "and shayshay back to El Grande. I reckon thet half o' map never left the Santa Alicia."

"Jose . . ." began Texas.

"Shore. Thet snakeroo!"

"But, durn it, Andrew Platt had the half an' those ginks took him away."

"Mebbe they took him away, but never saw the map. Mebbe it was dropped."

"Yeah?"

"And mebbe thet oily skunk, Jose Petrillio, got a-ho'd on it," snarled Krafton Webber.

Texas rubbed his Colt menacingly against the rock.

"Ef thet gent has the two halves . . ." he did not finish the sentence.

"Wal, we're podners with Jose, ain't we?" sneered Webber. "Hell, I'll show him what happens to a snake! Doggone it, we got to git out o' hyar!"

But there was no chance. The horses were in the distance, cropping at some grass. They were far enough to be undisturbed by any shooting. And they were far enough to be completely out of reach of any man making a dash for it. Anyone who started to run would be asking for a steel-jacketed slug from the law-men's rifles.

After some exchange of Colt fire for Winchester bullets, the affray became quiet. The five outlaws hugged the hot rock. They huddled down in the shelter of their particular rocky basin. Heat beat at them. They hardly dared move. One man darted less than three yards to a better hole and drew cracking shots from across the flat.

After about an hour of the dogged fight, thirst began to play havoc with the outlaws. The water canteens were on the saddles. Just to think of water made them gasp with the dust in their throats.

Heat hazes shimmered all around and seemed to suggest movements ahead. But the movements were not real. Staring into the heat hazes was hard on the eyes and a strain on tempers.

Texas Callahan licked dry lips.

"Hell, do we squat hyar till night?"

"Mebbe," grunted Krafton Webber.

But Rork Doonan had other ideas.

He was well placed, with a maze of boulders to his back. It was possible for him to withdraw without showing himself much.

The others could not cross to the boulders because they would have to dash over a patch of sand and shale. They could make the dash, but they would risk a shot from the rifles across the flat.

Rork Doonan crept from boulder to boulder and gradually got away. After a few minutes he was sufficiently far away to start running. He had to make a wide detour to get around to the spot where the horses were cropping.

Finally, he reached his own horse. He jumped to the saddle and then moved to round up the other animals.

Inside a few minutes he had them all on a lead rope. Looking back, he saw the red bluffs where the law-men were holed-up. They were about half a mile away.

Rork Doonan had plenty of reckless courage. He had been in with three owl-hoot bands in three States, and was a wanted man by several sheriffs.

He pulled his Winchester from the saddle-boot. He jigged the remuda through the winding paths between the humps of rock and shale hillocks.

As he got nearer to the red bluffs he decided to race past and on to the boulder-strewn land where the outlaws were hiding.

He got the horses moving fastly, and he hugged the neck of his mount.

As he approached the red bluffs, he began firing his rifle. He pumped a few shells at some rocks which he thought hid the law-men. He reloaded, still swaying expertly low in the saddle.

Winchesters roared back at him. He returned the fire, and fed steel to the horse. In a minute he had galloped past the red bluffs, unhurt because of the speed of the pounding horse.

His actions had one good result for Krafton Webber and his cohorts.

As Jed Ryland and Ezra Strang turned momentarily to fire at Rork Doonan, the other outlaws seized the chance they had waited hours for. They jumped back, over the dangerous patch of shale and sand, and hit the cover of the boulder maze in a few frantic seconds.

Then Rork Doonan sped by, the remuda of horses galloping close behind him.

Jed Ryland and Ezra Strang snapped off shots at the rocks which had hidden the outlaws, only to realise that the men had moved. There was no answering fire from the out-ranged Colts.

Desperately, Webber and his men scattered swiftly through the boulder maze. The holes gave cover for the leaping, running men.

Jed Ryland and Ezra came after them. The two law-men ran over the patch of flat land and entered the strewn boulders. Winchesters whipped up frequently to take snap shots at the fleeing outlaws. But the targets were only momentary. Then the men would dive to the clefts and scramble along to appear somewhere else for a fraction of a second. But shots rang out from Jed Ryland's rifle. All at once he saw one man leap and sprawl. The outlaw would never run again. He had stopped the bullet.

But Rork Doonan had raced the horses to a convenient spot and then waited for Krafton Webber and the others to run up.

Within minutes the static fight had changed to one of movement.

Krafton Webber, Texas Callahan and the breed reached Rork Doonan and the horses. They had left one man among the rocks. They swung to saddle leather. Horses wheeled and thundered back for El Grande in a swift rataplan of hoofs.

"Say, ain't we got time to mix it with

Ryland and thet blamed sheriff?" yelled
Texas Callahan.

"Aw, blast them hombres! I figger to
ketch up with Jose Petrillio. Say, we been
away from thet town nearly six hours!"

"Yuh figger—"

"I figger Jose Petrillio's got six hours
and more head-start!" shouted Webber.

"Yuh talk as though thet jigger had the
whole map."

"Wal, podner, we'll soon find out. Yep,
I reckon we'll soon find out!"

And the four horsemen thundered over
the flats, dust rising from hoofs. They
wheeled the horses round rocky outcrops
and were lost to sight. They were heading
back to El Grande—and more trouble.

They had left two dead rannigans in the
dry-gulch tangle with the law-men, but
this price did not bother Krafton Webber
in the slightest. He had gotten out of a
bad spot, and that was all that mattered
so far.

11

JED RYLAND and Ezra Strang watched the outlaws rowel horses into headlong flight. Jed, in particular, was staring keenly. He identified the fleeing men, and knew that Webber and Texas had got away. Then, the next second, the owl-hoots were lost in the jagged contours of the land.

"Let's git back for our hosses!" grunted Ezra. "Let's git after those hellions!"

Jed Ryland swung around, strode with the sheriff back to the cleft where they had tethered their horses. With hat pushed back to reveal straw-coloured hair and his blue eyes snapping angrily, Jed Ryland looked a big grim man.

"Tarnation! They slipped out o' thet dry-gulch! Thet tricky hombre with the hosses shore took my eyes off the main bunch."

"Reckon they're hittin' back to El Grande," muttered Ezra Strang.

They reached the horses. Ezra placed a hand on the saddle-horn and leaped to the leather. From his height on the saddle, he looked down at Jed with narrowed, thoughtful eyes.

"Kin yuh believe all thet about Webber havin' only half o' thet map?"

"Sounded kinda convincing," returned Jed. He tightened the cinch, and then leaped lithely to the saddle. "Shore sounded like he was puzzled as us. Appears the map got torn in half before thet gun-play in the room. Shore never reckoned on thet. I thought Webber had Andrew Platt's map."

"He cayn't find the gold with half a map!" rapped Ezra.

They jigged the horses into a gallop and headed for El Grande.

"Nope. Shore cayn't find the bonanza wi' half a map," said Jed calmly. "But thet don't say Webber won't find the second half. We still got to bring thet hombre in for a trial and a hang noose."

"Shore. An' I reckon we're jest about over the border which kinda makes us jest two hombres without any authority."

"Call us bounty hunters," said Jed grimly. "And the authority we got is right hyar in these guns!"

"Shore is enough for me!" muttered Sheriff Ezra Strang.

There was some hard riding before they sighted El Grande. The lawless Mexican town huddled together and looked more like a mirage in the afternoon heat. Jed Ryland and Ezra Strang rode in and marvelled at the smells and somnulence of the place. But they had keen eyes for sign of Krafton Webber and his cohorts. They rode past the Santa Alicia and went right through the main drag on the lookout for the wanted men. But there was no clue to the men's whereabouts.

"Guess we'll have to make a parley with thet crooked cuss, Jose Petrillio," muttered Ezra. "Mebbe he kin tell us if those jiggers rode through."

They rode back to the cantina. They

hitched the horses to the tie-rail, clumped over the boards and went inside.

A few ugly looks came their way, but that was all. They got a reply from a breed server.

"Sheriff Petrillio is busy at the sheriff's office, señors."

They made their way out. Jed Ryland watched the upper windows of the two-story building, but saw no suspicious signs.

"Let's go ask questions in the livery," grunted Ezra Strang. "The wrangler might ha' seen Webber an' his galoots ride in."

"All right. We pass the livery on the way down."

They found the old Mexican wrangler and rapped questions about any strangers who had ridden into town. They got a reply in Spanish. It was as well Jed Ryland and Ezra knew the language fairly well.

"Señors, the men you want are in jail."

Jed Ryland stared.

"Jail? How's that?" he asked in the lingo.

"They ride into town, amigo, and Sheriff Petrillio and two posse-men hold guns on them after a short talk. The sheriff knows the law. So these hombres are put in jail and guns taken away. Jose Petrillio say they are wanted men. I do not know."

Jed and Ezra walked on their way, leading the animals.

"Wal, we shore know they're wanted men," observed Jed. "This is shore a change from Jose Petrillio's earlier attitude. Thet greaser was playing ball with Webber at first—hidin' him an' warning him about us moseying around! Now he throws 'em in the hoosegow!"

"I reckon we're on our way to see Sheriff Jose Petrillio," said Ezra grimly. "Mebbe he'll hand over those galoots for trial in Monument City."

"Mebbe," said Jed.

The sheriff's office in El Grande was situated next to a stone-built jail. The whole building was in the town square.

The jail looked very substantial. Any one could walk up and look through the barred windows, if they wished to. Not many would because it could be dangerous sport. The few ruffians who languished in the hoosegow as prisoners on the whim of the law had no weapons, but they had fists. Two fists could reach out and strangle anyone who fooled around near the barred windows.

Jed Ryland found Jose Petrillio sitting in a big chair at a desk and looking very sleepy. The sheriff had his badge pinned to his shirt. He had discarded his jacket. He carried his two guns in the approved manner, low on the thighs.

When the Texas Ranger and his partner entered Jose Petrillio looked up and smiled sleepily.

Jed came straight to the point.

"We've ridden back for those rannigans, Sheriff Petrillio. We hear you've got 'em in the jail-house."

"Who tell you?" asked Jose Petrillio softly.

"Forget thet!" snapped Jed. "All right,

288

when kin we ride them jiggers back for trial?"

Jose Petrillio shrugged.

"Señors, you have the wrong idea. These men start a disturbance in El Grande, smash up property. They break things in my cantina. They will be tried in El Grande, amigo."

"If yuh escort them to the border under a posse, we kin take over," snapped Jed. "These men are wanted for murder. What d'yuh figger to stick on 'em? Thirty days for making a disturbance?"

Jose Petrillio drew himself to his feet and tried to speak impressively.

"This is Mexico, señors. We try these men and maybe hand them to you—who knows?"

Jed snapped angry blue eyes at him, and Jose Petrillio drew back somewhat.

"Lissen, yuh got some queer ideas, Sheriff Petrillio! What goes on with yuh? Mebbe yuh tangled yore play with these hellions, huh?"

"I tell you they have broken the law!

For that they will be punished. They will stay in jail, amigo. That is final."

"Kin we see them an' mebbe talk to them?" asked Ezra Strang.

"Don't refuse thet!" snapped Jed. "Or mebbe we might report yuh to some gink a bit higher up in this blamed country. Ezra Strang is sheriff of Monument City an' a neighbouring town even if it is across the border. I'm a Texas Ranger. We got a right to question these men. Do we get it?"

Jose Petrillio spread his hands.

"Sure, amigo, sure! I lead the way, please!"

A door at the back of the office led to a passage and then a room. A vaquero with a deputy badge and a steeple-shaped hat was sitting on a chair. He was whittling a bit of wood. On both sides of the room were cells with iron gates. The Mexican deputy got up as Jose Petrillio entered.

"These the men you speak about?" inquired Jose Petrillio.

Jed Ryland smiled grimly at the other's

unctuous manner. He stared at the cells swiftly, saw Krafton Webber in one. Texas Callahan was glowering from behind the bars of another. Jed knew the man called Rork Doonan. He was closeted with the half-breed.

"Shore, these are the gents," returned Jed. "Wal, hello, Webber! Yuh shore rode back into trouble when yuh left those two jiggers of yourn dead in the broken country. So yuh let Sheriff Petrillio git the drop on yuh?"

"What d'yuh want?" snarled Webber.

"Wal, we want to ride yuh back to Monument fer trial. Jest tryin' to persuade Jose to let yuh go—with a posse escort."

Krafton Webber breathed heavily.

"Mighty fine talk, Ryland. Hell, I wish I could git a gun on yuh, snake!"

Jed Ryland narrowed his eyes.

"Thet's an idee . . . Wal, now, Webber, yuh told me yuh had half o' thet map. I kinda believe yuh. Let me see thet half. I'm mighty interested."

Webber rattled the bars in a spasm of rage.

"Say, lissen, Jose, git thet hombre out o' hyar! We kin talk business! We—"

Krafton Webber broke off and rasped into harsh noises as he realised he had nearly said too much.

"Mebbe yuh kin show me yore half o' the map," snapped Jed Ryland.

"I ain't doin' business with a skunk."

"Wal, I ain't got to be so particular. Who has the other half o' the map, Webber?" asked Jed shrewdly.

"It was lost, I reckon."

"Yeah? That means the gold is lost. How'd yuh like thet idee?"

"Purty bad," commented Krafton Webber.

"Yeah. Wal, in thet case yuh should have no objection to me seein' yore half o' the map. Howsabout it?"

"Yuh kin go to hell!" snarled Webber. "Yuh jiggers got no authority over hyar. Git them out o' hyar, Jose."

Jose Petrillio smiled.

"You hear, señors? It is true. Now you

have talked, please to leave. This is El Grande, amigos."

"It shore is El Grande," rapped Ezra Strang. "I couldn't git away with this in Monument City!"

"You have spoken to the prisoners, señors. Please to go now!"

"How'd yuh like us to poke a gun at yuh?" asked Jed gravely.

Something flickered over Jose Petrillio's eyes.

"But you cannot do that, amigo. You have a great respect for the law. These hombres are being held by El Grande with serious charges against them. Now if you play for your guns, you will make things very bad. Perhaps I will have to send a report to the Governor of Texas."

Jed turned away.

"Forget it, Jose. I was kinda kidding. Wal, guess we'll mosey along and stop by in one o' the cantinas."

As they walked out of the jail-house there was complete silence. Krafton Webber glowered, but Jose Petrillio merely smiled.

When Jed and Ezra had gone, Webber snarled:

"All right, yuh got us tangled in yore loop, Jose. Yuh got the map. All right, all right, so yuh won't say yuh have the map! Lemme tell yuh somethin', Jose— yuh'll need some hard hombres to track thet bonanza. Yuh c'd make a deal with us. Like I said afore. Yuh keep one half o' the map, an' I'll keep the other. We'll set off for the Guadalupes with no guns. No guns anywhere, Jose! Yuh keep one half o' the map! I keep the other. We c'd track the mine like that. Wi' no guns at all, yuh got a guarantee o' no tricky play. Hell, when we find the gold, there'll be enough for everybody!".

"I shall think about it," said Jose Petrillio smoothly. "And for now you stay right here, señors. Do not make a noise! Do not think you can escape. You are creeminals. I tell yuh, huh? Yes, I have the full map, amigos. I picked one half off the floor of the room in my cantina! Now I go."

The vaquero on guard sat down when

Jose Petrillio went out. The man had heard nothing. He went on whittling his wood. He could not hear anything because he was deaf and dumb, and Jose Petrillio had chosen this unusual deputy for those very reasons.

But the two other rannigans were far from deaf and dumb. In fact, they had extraordinary good hearing.

When the talking stopped Jed Ryland stopped listening at the barred window from outside the jailhouse, and looked through swiftly. Then he walked away slowly.

Ezra Strang came after him with the peculiar roll of a man who spent long hours in the saddle.

"So Jose Petrillio has the whole map," mused Jed. "Thet durned map shore gits around! So he picked one half off the floor at the Santa Alicia! Wal, ain't we the dumb goons! Andrew Platt must ha' dropped it or it got knocked from his hand. Heck, I should ha' seen it!"

"Don't be too hard on yoreself," grunted Ezra.

"Wal, it don't rightly matter. I jest got the idee thet the hombre who Injuned up on Webber and slugged him the other night must ha' bin Jose. Couldn't be anyone else, now thet we know what's bin goin' on. Jose rustled one half o' the map from Webber. Then thet gink figgered we had one half. An' we figgered Webber had the whole map."

"Sounds too durned mixed fer me!" growled Ezra. "I heerd thet oily no-good sheriff say he had the whole map. Thet's enough, podner. He's keeping Webber in the hoosegow jest to suit himself. Mebbe he figgers to organise a party and light out fer the gold soon. A party of durned vaqueros, I reckon."

"Unless he makes a deal with Webber," commented Jed.

"He'll make a deal with a rattler, iffen he does!"

"Wal, the play ain't over yet."

They walked over to the horses, untied the reins.

"Yuh got any idees?" asked Ezra in a hushed voice.

"Yep. But they're all illegal."

"I don't give a hoot—" began Ezra.

"I guessed yuh didn't, podner. Iffen we cayn't act in the law in this blamed country, we'll act out of it."

"Shore. As long as yuh tell me what yuh figger on doing!"

"Wal, it's simple. We jest git thet map —whole this time. An' then we organise a jail-break for Webber and his pals."

"Thet's a new one fer me," grunted Ezra.

"Mebbe. But Webber and his hell-bents won't git far."

Because there was no real rush, they led the horses along to a cantina and hitched them to the rail. Then they went inside the place. They got a table far from the sallow-faced vaqueros who lolled against the counter drinking and smoking brown-paper cigarettes. They could talk in low tones.

For the rest of the stifling afternoon, Jed Ryland and Sheriff Ezra Strang seemed to be as indolent as the tilma-wearing Mexicans. They rested in the cool interior of the cantina. After some time they took the horses along to the Mexican liveryman for feed and water, but that was their only activity. Then, when the sun went down like a red ball of fire, they went out to the Chinese eathouse. They had steak and wondered where it had been rustled. After that they went along for the horses.

It was dark now, and the only lights were the yellow patches which came from the saloons and gambling joints on the main stem. Jed and Ezra led the animals in the pale moonlight, and hitched them to a tie-rail convenient to the square, squat jail-house.

Just fifty yards away was the Santa Alicia saloon, where Jose Petrillio was very probably located.

"All right, we go git the map off Jose," muttered Jed. "If he won't hand over, we threaten to kill him or somethin'!"

"Thet should be easy," snapped Ezra.

"He's a hard customer. He mightn't give in easy. Wal, let's git—" Jed broke off sharply.

Staring over at the darkness all around the square jail-house, Jed Ryland thought he saw a figure move. It was not much. It was simply a movement of darkness against the deeper, velvety blackness of the jail-house wall.

But Jed Ryland acted on his hunch. The same hunches had operated in his life before, and sometimes led him to raw action and sometimes to safety.

Without a word, he stepped away swiftly, leaving Ezra Strang. In seconds, he reached the deep gloom around the jail-house wall. Another three seconds and his long arm snaked out to stop a murder play.

Jed Ryland tightened his hand around the gun thrust through the barred window of the jail. With his other arm, he forced the man backwards away from the prison.

He had known it was a man who had moved up swiftly in the night. His hunch had told him to expect danger.

The man was Mexican, dressed in shapeless, hanging tilma and steeple-shaped hat. He had had a gun pointed at the prisoners in the jail-house. Jed Ryland could guess why.

But thoughts were swept away in a savage struggle. The man tried to bring his gun up to bear on Jed. One bone-breaking twist, and Jed had forced the gun out of the man's hand. The weapon fell to the dusty road. Then the man tried to writhe away, out of Jed Ryland's grip.

Jed rammed a solid punch to the vaquero's jaw. The man staggered back, fell to his hands and knees and then tried to slither away.

Jed Ryland jumped forward, grabbed the man's clothes and hoisted him to his feet. Jed punished the hombre with two blows that jerked the man's head back on his neck as if it was loose. Then Jed just held the man up. All the fight was out of the fellow.

"All right, talk! Who told yuh to plug those fellers in the hoosegow? Speak, durn yuh!"

Jed Ryland wanted some corroboration, that was all. He had a darned good idea who wanted Krafton Webber and his side-kicks out of the way.

Ezra rolled up out of the dark night and laid big hands on the man. Jed Ryland jerked out words of explanation. Then he shook the vaquero as if he was an old mat.

"Who hired yuh? Was it Jose Petrillio?"

The man gasped, rolled his eyes whitely. He seemed too scared to speak. All at once Jed thrust the man to the dusty road again.

"Git goin'. Yuh better light out o' town, hombre. Jose won't like to hear yuh failed him. Git!"

Like an animal, the man scrambled away on all fours. Then he got to his feet and disappeared in the dark.

Jed took Ezra's arm and together they walked up to the barred windows of the hoosegow. Jed stopped at one, changed his mind and walked slowly to the other. He did not stretch up to look in.

"Kin yuh hear me, Webber?"

A voice growled back immediately.

"Shore. What the hell d'yuh want?"

"Nothin' much. Jest figgered to tell yuh your pal, Jose Petrillio, was ready to send a hombre to fill yuh with lead."

Krafton Webber's voice sounded nearer, as if he had got up and approached the window.

"Are yuh crazy? What d'yuh mean?"

"Jest thet we found a jigger poking a gun through these windows," said Jed patiently. "One o' Jose's men, I'll be bound. Nice o' him, wasn't it?"

Webber cursed.

"So thet greaser wants to rub us out! Thet's his ornery idee in keepin' us hyar! Ryland, git us out o' hyar! Git us out afore thet skunk kills us!"

"Some feller killin' yuh doesn't worry me none," snapped Jed. "But I aim to see yuh dangle legally. We'll be back— to-night, Webber!"

As Jed and Ezra walked away, they heard the rattle of bars in cement sockets as the prisoners shook them furiously.

Jed and the sheriff walked steadily over to the Santa Alicia cantina. With hands

302

that dangled like scoops near to their gun-butts, they walked through the batwing doors, past the group of talking, gesticulating vaqueros and towards the stairway.

One of the white bartenders saw them go up. He was about to reach for a shotgun which lay propped against the pine counter. He saw Jed Ryland half-turn and place hands on Colt-butts. The bartender seized a cloth and began swabbing instead. He muttered to himself.

With a thin smile, Jed continued upward. With Ezra, he went down the passage, past the room which had seen the fighting in which Andrew Platt had been killed.

They found a door which was marked "Private" but which was hanging badly on twisted hinges. Jed did not know that Texas Callahan had broken the door. He gave the matter no thought. The door was obviously unable to lock. With one hand he pushed the door open and strode in.

Jose Petrillio was sitting at a table studying a map of the Texas-Mexico border between Laredo, Monument City and the Guadalupe Mountains. One glance at the map told Jed Ryland plenty. He recognised the locations on the map.

"Plannin' a trip, Jose?" he asked.

The sheriff of El Grande looked at the twin Colts which lay so nonchalantly in the big, fair-haired man's hands. Then he looked at steely blue eyes. Jose Petrillio tried to smile. He looked sideways to Ezra Strang, saw a bristling moustache and grim grey eyes under a trail-dusty hat.

"Howdy, amigos. Please put the guns away. We have no need of guns."

"Keep yore hands on the table," advised Jed. "I ain't puttin' these hoglegs away until we git thet map of yuh, Jose Petrillio. An' we want it whole, amigo. Yuh savvy, huh? We know the full play now."

Jose Petrillio shrugged. He was wearing his store suit because the night was always cool in comparison to the day. He had a flowered shirt and a black necktie around the collar. His sheriff's badge was pinned to the coat. The man's thick greasy hair gave him a powerful appearance, but in reality Jose Petrillio had a yellow streak.

"I do not keep the map here, señors," said Jose coolly. "If yuh kill me, the map is lost. No one will know where to look. And yuh cannot kill me. I am the sheriff of El Grande. I am the friend of the county Judge. Even the Governor knows me. You would hang if you killed me."

"Cut out the fancy word-play!" snarled Ezra. "Whar's thet durned map? Hand over and mebbe we kin git back to a respectable country! Yuh ain't fittin to be a sheriff, yuh low-down crook!"

Jed Ryland smiled serenely. He was not a bit worried. He figured he had some tricks to deal with snakeroo Jose Petrillio!

"We want thet map and we want Webber and his podners," he said. "The map will go back to Monument City and if Andrew Platt has heirs, it will be their property. If not, the location of the bonanza will be State property. The State will disclose the location of the gold to everyone on a given date and then it will be up to prospectors to journey out and file claims for themselves. I guess thet will start a bit o' a gold rush, but thet's bin the procedure before. So hand over thet map. Neither yuh nor Webber and his cohorts got any right to it."

"I theenk you want the gold for yourself!" sneered Jose Petrillio.

"I've seen gold rushes," rapped Jed. "Any jigger who kin git gold out o' them durned wildernesses is entitled to it. I ain't in any hurry to git my hands on gold. I'm more interested in my job. Aw, shucks to words. Whar's the map?"

"It is hidden," said Jose silkily.

"Whar?"

"I will not tell you, amigo, an' you will not kill me. You are law-men. You cannot kill just because I will not give you the map. That is not your law, amigo. No! You can put your guns away, señor, and walk back to your horses. Perhaps I do not know anything about maps, huh?"

And Jose began to smile again.

Jed Ryland smiled grimly. Ezra just glared.

"All right," rapped Jed. "Yuh figger

yuh're smart hombre. All right, feller. I'll count ten an' if yuh don't hand over thet map I figger to set this dump on fire. Get it?"

"You—you—cannot do that!" stammered Jose.

"I shore kin. An' if the durned map's in this saloon an' gits burned, it ain't goin' to worry us none. Platt's bonanza will be jest another lost gold mine. The west's full o' 'em! What with crazy prospectors and Injun mines, that's enough gold out hyar to make everyone rich—when they durned well find the stuff! Okay, Jose, I'm goin' to start counting."

And Jed Ryland began in grim earnest. "One . . . two . . . three . . ."

Jose Petrillio darted sweaty glances from Ezra to Jed. In Ezra Strang he saw a hard, lined face of a just man who knew his own mind. In Jed Ryland, he saw a younger man but with the same implacable sense of justice. It was the desire for justice above all things—justice and freedom—which had made the west. And the men who brought it about were hard men.

". . . four . . . five . . . six . . ."

Jose Petrillio really perspired.

"Señors, I tell you, the map it is not here. You cannot burn this cantina . . ."

He half-rose. His hands were near his guns. It was sheer instinct. Jed stopped counting to rap:

"Go for them smokepoles, amigo, an' I shoot in self-defence."

That stopped Jose Petrillio. Jed began counting again.

". . . seven . . . eight . . . nine . . ."

"You cannot burn my cantina! You cannot keel me! I will have my hombres shoot you!" spat Jose Petrillio.

"For the last time—the map!"

Jose Petrillio hesitated, unwilling to believe the worst. He figured the other was bluffing.

"Ten!" snapped Jed Ryland.

He immediately grabbed at the oil-lamp which stood on the table beside the printed map. He whipped out a riding glove and slipped it on. He took off the glass in a second and began to spill oil over the floor.

The next instant the lamp was dashed to the ground. Oil ran all over the place. The red-hot wick ignited the oil in a second. Like magic, flames leaped up and licked at wood furniture and rugs.

"Thet's the end o' Platt's map!" rasped Jed Ryland. "And your saloon will be ashes for your trickery!"

Jose Petrillio roared in alarm. He threw himself forward and tried to stamp out the flames. Oil clung to his suit and burned it. He had to back away from the red, oily sheets of flame. Already the wood wall was crackling into flame.

"Fool! Fool! Now I lose everything!"

"If the map's in hyar, git it afore it's too late!" rapped Jed.

With rage contorting his swarthy face, Jose Petrillio blundered past the two lawmen. Then he turned.

"Cursed fools! The map is in a drawer of that table! It cannot be got out now. I must get my vaqueros to stamp out this fire!"

As if on the same impulse, Jed and Ezra stepped forward to get closer to the writing-table. Flames beat at them. There was a stink of burning oil and wood.

They tried for fully a minute to get closer to the table, but scorching heat was filling the room. Red flames licked past them, threatening to trap them. The fire was spreading. Already smoke and flames were gushing out into the passage.

Jed took Ezra's arm.

"Let's git out o' hyar!"

"If the map's gorn, thet's the end o' it!" gasped Ezra.

They lurched out of the fire-filled room, rocked on their heels a bit as they coughed.

Men were racing up the stairs. Jed showed his guns, and Ezra too, and the vaqueros fell back to allow the two men passage. Jed and Ezra raced down the stairs. From the cantina floor, now empty of men, they looked back. They saw fire swirling along the passage at the top of the stairs, heard the ominous crack of sparks.

"They cayn't put out this fire!" gasped Ezra. "They ain't got nuthin' in this town to put out fires."

"Thet's the end o' the map!" said Jed grimly.

They strode out into the night, pushed through a crowd of breeds and went swiftly to the jail-house. They rapped on the door with gun-butts, and when the door swung open to the touch they got a shock of suspicion. They walked inside and found the cells were empty. Webber and his men had gone!

12

JED RYLAND went all around the jail-house. Not only had Krafton Webber, Texas Callahan, Rork Doonan and the breed vanished, but the deputy was not to be seen either.

Then Jed went through the door that connected the jail with Sheriff Petrillio's office.

He looked around keenly. There were things he noted in a flash.

A saddle was missing from the place where he had noticed it the last time. A rifle had been taken from the rack of three.

"Thet jigger's ridin' out!" he snapped. "Heck, I wonder if the coyote has tricked us!"

Ezra turned a puzzled face to the younger man.

"What d'yuh mean?"

Jed wiped sweat from his neck with the yellow bandanna.

"Jose Petrillio let those hombres free. Now why? It wasn't because he wanted to. Nope! He wanted to use 'em, thet's all! Remember thet deal we overheard Webber stack up for Jose Petrillio? Mebbe thet's it. Thar ain't no other reason why Petrillio should let Webber and his rannigans out."

"Yuh figger Jose Petrillio still has the map?" jerked Ezra.

"Could be. What if thet tricky jigger had the map hidden down hyar?"

"Goldarn it, yuh're tellin' me thet pesky map is still being thrown around!" roared Ezra.

"I shore hoped it was burned," said Jed grimly. "But if the map didn't exist any more, Jose wouldn't let Webber an' his side-kicks free to fill him with lead. Nope. Thet cuss raced down hyar, got the map and figgered it best to make a deal with Webber. I guess they've rode out."

Ezra started for the door.

"Ef thet jigger made a deal with

Webber, it's because he figgers they can find the gold as a party. Mebbe they've set off now?"

"Mebbe. Let's git to those hosses."

When they raced outside, the night air was filled with a red glow from the burning cantina. A huge crowd was lining the road. Sparks were flying in all directions. As Jed Ryland and Ezra Strang shouldered forward to the tie-rail some distance from the doomed saloon, they heard the heavy crash of falling wood beams. The Santa Alicia was destined to be ashes!

They got the horses, mounted to the saddle and jigged them away.

"Wal, I ain't wastin' sympathy on thet crooked gent!" growled Ezra.

"Mebbe this town will git a new sheriff," commented Jed. "Thet hombre shore thinks quick. I guess he losin' plenty in this fire. He knows thet an' figgers to start on the gold hunt. Yep. Shore a fast thinker!"

Hoofs beat a tattoo as they rode out of town. Once clear of the adobe and wood shacks, they slackened pace and conferred about their bearings.

"We cayn't track them jiggers," said Jed Ryland. "Thet old moon don't give enough light, and thar's too many hoof-prints around this land. Nope! I guess those jiggers are makin' for the Guada-lupes right now. What do yuh think, podner?"

"I guess yuh're right." Ezra nodded, sitting upright in the saddle, staring around the flat moonlit terrain. "But they cayn't have got much time to git a lot o' gear. Mebbe they got no guns, like Jose Petrillio figgered?"

"Mebbe. I don't know. I shore wouldn't like to ride up into the Guada-lupes without a gun. Yuh git slinking mountain lions, rattlers, eagles . . ."

"Wal, I guess we kin catch up on them afore they hit those mountains," said Ezra. He pointed to a dark distant range of hills, just discernible against the wan light of the new moon and scudding clouds. "We take a trail through thar, I reckon. Git through them hills and we kin see the Guadalupes by daylight. Reckon those mountains are about seventy miles from hyar. Jest inside the border. Matter o' fact, Monument City is kinda nearer to the Guadalupes, but it's a different direction. Wal, if we ride for them hills, we kin catch up with those galoots. We still want those jiggers for murder and robbery."

And that was the way they saw it. If the hunt required more riding, they would go on until something happened. One thing, the trail was taking hunted and hunter back into Texas territory. If Jed and Ezra had no other asset in the arid land, they would have law on their side. But the law would need Colt fire!

It was as well they had rested the horses during the day and fed them at the livery, for as they rode on the moon climbed the sky and the hours and miles slipped away. The foothills rose to enfold them, and still there was no sign of Krafton Webber and his cohorts or their new partner, Jose Petrillio. After a while two tired men rode grimly and silently into a canyon with a silvery bed. In the moonlight, brighter now, they could see the other end and the natural trail which wound up a rocky slope covered with scrub.

The horses plodded on over the silvery sand. For almost three miles the virgin sand lay over the canyon bed. The hills provided a blanket which ensured utter silence in the canyon. It was ghostly, but to the two saddle-weary men no new experience.

They let the horses take their own time. It was crazy to rowel them to anything faster. In this desert, they were actually utterly dependent on the animals.

Only the creek of saddle leather, the jingle of spurs and heavy breathing of the two horses made a sound.

Unexpectedly, as if to make grim contrast, a gunshot cracked the night air!

The sound was distant and must have travelled miles. The horses took no notice of the unexpected sound. But Jed Ryland and Ezra Strang sat upright in the saddles and peered sharply all around.

"Cayn't be anyone else in this perishin' land but us an' them hellions!" barked Ezra.

"Seems like one o' 'em got a gun!" commented Jed.

They dropped further talk to listen. Once again it was almost intolerably silent in the canyon. No other sounds came to their ears except the noises made by their own horses and movement.

"One shot," mused Jed, at last. "A Colt shot, I guess. Might have bin thet direction."

And he pointed to the west, to a huddle of saw-toothed ridges. They were about two miles from the canyon they were traversing.

"Yeah? I wonder who got kilt?" barked Ezra.

"Mebbe no one got killed," returned Jed, with a wide smile.

Ezra looked disappointed. He fell to muttering.

"Wal, they cayn't kill each other with one shot!"

It was obvious they had got some lead

on the outlaws. At the risk of laming the horses, they jugged them to a canter. They travelled down the canyon and urged the animals up the steep shale slope. The horses had to spring and dig gamely with hoofs to climb the slope. But they got to the ridge and halted momentarily to stare ahead.

There was no obvious sign of the renegades, so they rode down the other side of the shale slope to a narrow valley congested with gaunt Joshua trees. As the horses avoided clumps of silvery cholla cactus, the riders looked for sign. The moon was really bright enough to enable them to see a trail if and when they got on to it.

A mile ahead they found it.

The natural trail led through the hills, and any rider wanting to go in that direction just had to use the flat portions of land. They came on the imprint of horses' hoofs imbedded in the sandy waste of the trail. To their expert eyes, they were fresh imprints. The trail was definitely clear now. The outlaws had ridden up by a different route, going along by another valley. But now they were on their trail. They guessed they would have found the outlaws' trail in time. The gunshot had helped.

A mile further down the twisting valley as it snaked through red-faced, crumbling hills, they hit upon a spring. Horses had watered at the spring and the water was still muddy through the churning hoofs. The outlaws were certainly not far ahead.

Jed and Ezra stopped to fill their own canteens and then let their horses have a fair drink. They rowelled the animals away before they got too much.

They rode after the trail again, finding the tell-tale hoof-prints every few yards. Even when the trail went over hard rock, they knew it would appear again a bit further on.

They eventually got their first glimpse of the five men as they rode over a ridge. They were outlined against the pale sky.

"Shore looks like no one got kilt!" said Ezra, disgruntled.

Jed Ryland merely maintained his fixed, serene smile.

From that moment they kept to the dark shadows thrown by the hills. All the time they reckoned they were gaining on the unsuspecting outlaws.

They finally caught up with the men when the outfit rode into a blind canyon and had to turn to ride through a natural tunnel in the canyon wall. The tunnel had been carved by eroding winter winds which carried sand and rain. For centuries the erosion had taken place until a grotesque bore in the canyon wall had developed into a tunnel.

As the five riders turned and rode into the tunnel, Jed and Ezra came up within shooting range. The horses were moving at a canter. Jed Ryland was the first to fire at the black figures of the moving horsemen.

Crack!

The canyon walls reverberated with the shot. A man ahead in the pale light cried and then cursed with pain. In a second, the renegade horsemen had jabbed spurs to flanks and the horses leaped into the darkness of the tunnel. They were gone.

Ezra Strang lowered his gun. There was not a worthwhile target. He fed spur steel to his mount, and the horse sprang to a gallop.

"Let's git after 'em!" he bawled. "I figger yuh got one rat!"

The two law-men rowelled horses into the comparative darkness of the natural tunnel. The high roof arched overhead. Jed saw the last of the fleeing horsemen turning the corner. He and Ezra pumped a shot after them. But they were just chance shots, and got no answering yell of pain. There were no retaliatory shots, either.

Through the tunnel and over a stretch of flat shale and cactus, and then Jed and Ezra were riding down a narrow rock-bound gully little more than wide enough for two horses abreast and with walls fully thirty feet high. Just ahead were the desperately riding outlaws. The two law-men pumped more shots after them, but they apparently went wide owing to the leaping and twisting of the horses as they strove to avoid rocks and holes.

The narrow gully twisted and gave cover to the outlaws. Jed and Ezra rounded a sharp turn—and then a gun roared at them and flame stabbed the darkness.

Jed realised instinctively that this was a deadly ambush. It was a natural for a dry-gulch. Simultaneously with this thought, he heard Ezra's gasp of pain. Jed reined in, bringing the horse almost to its haunches. He roared to Ezra to wheel his horse. As the animals turned with a plunging of hoofs in the narrow gully, a gun cracked again. The slug whined over Jed's head. He whipped a gun over his shoulder and fired backwards, stabbing hot lead and flame into the dry-gulch just to deter the attacker.

The next second they were safely around the sharp bend. Solid rock hid them from the dry-gulcher.

"Say, podner, yuh stopped a slug?" inquired Jed.

He leaned over from his horse. Ezra

was slumping in the saddle. He was clutching his side and almost buckling up. It was a wonder he still stuck to saddle leather.

"I got—one—podner!" he gasped.

"Is it bad?" rasped Jed.

"Bad enough—I reckon! Durn it—that —gink was—waitin' fer—us!"

Jed gritted his teeth. He realised the outlaws were getting farther away. But there was one man just around the bend of the gully. He was certainly taking on a risky job to protect his pals.

Jed took off his bandanna and then Ezra's. He shook the dust from them grimly. He tied them and then began to bind the crude bandage around Ezra's middle. He could see the patch of red on the sheriff's side. He was binding the bandage really tight when a voice hoarse with rage and pain shouted from somewhere in the gully ahead.

"Ain't yuh a-comin' on! Damnation take yuh, Ryland! Come on around hyar an' settle accounts. I got a slug a-waiting for yuh!"

It was Rork Doonan's voice. He was holed-up somewhere in the darkness ahead in the gully. Jed, listening grimly, heard the pain in his voice and guessed Rork Doonan was the man he had hit with a Colt slug.

"I'm comin'!" Jed snapped. "Jest sit thar an' wait. Yuh takin' all the chances, Doonan?"

There was a wild snarling laugh from the distant man. It was a laugh of utter recklessness, defiance and pain.

Then:

"Yuh got me, yuh blamed skunk! I stopped a bit o' lead, but I ain't packed in yet!" There was a pause and an audible gasp as the man strove for breath to shout again. "Jose Petrillio gave me the gun, the oily son-of-bitch! No guns, Ryland— how'd yuh like thet! No guns among us—'cept Jose Petrillio. Now I got the gun. Come on yuh durned mangy law-man! Come an' shoot it out! I hate all law-men! I jest hate yore guts, Ryland!"

"Yuh're dying, Doonan!" called Jed sternly. "I don't have to go gunning for yuh! I kin let yuh die. But I won't. I'm a-comin' for yuh, Doonan!"

Jed vaulted from his horse. He patted Ezra to stay put on his mount. Then he began to creep ahead.

He knew the chance he was taking. He was risking a shot ending his own life. The man ahead had nothing to lose. He would die horribly and slowly if left. But Jed Ryland felt a grim desire to pump lead and justice into the outlaw.

"I'm comin', Doonan!" he thundered. "I aim to finish yuh off!"

"Blast yuh!" screamed the man. "I'll git yuh! Shore as hell, I'll git yuh! I'll take yuh with me, Ryland! The other jiggers are gittin' away! No damned guns, though! Haw! Haw! No damned gold fer me! Gawd, I aim to git yuh!"

The man was almost crazy. He knew he was dying. Even if he killed Jed Ryland, he would die himself. He could not hoist himself on to a horse, let alone ride miles and miles! Only by a desperate effort had he kept on long enough to get the gun from Jose Petrillio. And that wily individual had seen the advantage . . .

"I'm a-comin', Doonan!" shouted Jed. "I'll finish yuh off, rat! Mebbe yuh can tell me somethin'? Mebbe yuh kin tell me who has the map?"

Jed slithered into a crevice just around the sharp bend. A shot whined angrily at him. Jed flattened and then whipped a gun up and snapped a shot at the other man.

"I kin tell yuh, Ryland!" taunted Rork Doonan. "Jest move agin, Ryland. Jest move! Shore, the map's shared out between Webber and Petrillio. Jose tried to kid us there weren't no guns until Webber tried to git the other half o' map from him. Then thet rattler pulled a gun out a' his pocket an' snapped a slug near enough to blow Webber's hat off! But those rannigans ain't got no guns now, haw, haw!"

Before the man stopped speaking, Jed Ryland dived fiercely for a rocky crag half-way up the gully wall. He reached it as lead bit all around him, missing him by inches. Jed smiled grimly. He had taken a great chance with that leap. It was just luck. A slug could have taken him. But now he had a commanding position over the gully. The next time Rork Doonan fired, he would get the man's exact location.

And Rork Doonan, prodded on by his killer lust even though he was dying, made the fatal move. He fired to the spot where he fancied Jed lurked. He raised himself to sight his gun . . .

Jed Ryland had his Colt resting on rock. As the other gun spat flame and lead, he drew a bead on the spot and triggered.

Rork Doonan, slowed by his wounds, did not flatten quickly enough after his chance shot. He missed Jed. But the lawman's shot killed him instantly. The slug took him in the head. He was thrown back under the impact and died.

Jed Ryland was not quite sure for some time. Then he called sternly to the other man.

He got no answer for the other had been dead a minute.

"Doonan! Kin yuh hear me? Want to try again, Doonan?"

Still no answer. But Jed knew silence was often a trick. There were rannigans who played possum.

But he chanced it. He moved and dodged back. When the other man did not fire, he knew it was all over. He had given the outlaw a first-class opportunity. Any gun-man would have taken it.

Jed Ryland climbed up and went over the rocky floor of the gully until he found Rork Doonan. The man was absolutely dead. He took the gun from the still tight fingers. Jed rammed it into his belt. Then he walked back rapidly to find Ezra Strang.

There was one thing. He knew Krafton Webber and his cohorts would be a long way off by now.

He found Ezra still propped on his horse. The sheriff was lolling in the saddle. When he saw Jed Ryland he barked:

"Doggone this bit o' lead! Shore busted the play. So yuh got thet varmint!"

"Yep. Say, Ezra, yuh got to git some doc to work over yuh. Kin yuh stick in thet saddle until we hit Monument City?"

"Mebbe, but yuh goin' after them outlaws. I kin ride back alone."

"Yuh old moseyhorn, yuh'll fall offen thet hoss afore yuh git half-way. Who'll stick yuh on again?"

"Yuh got a chance to catch up with them blamed owl-hoots!" argued Ezra. "They cayn't be more'n a few miles on an' they ain't got no guns. I heerd thet ornery galoot afore he died."

"It don't matter about Webber an' his pals. I know where those jiggers are headin'. Right for the gold. I reckon I can track 'em any time. I remember Andrew Platt's directions about the twin peaks an' the Injun trail. I kin find those galoots afore they find the bonanza—iffen they ever find the bonanza!"

"Mebbe them catamounts will never find the gold!" grunted Ezra.

Jed Ryland climbed to the saddle.

"They ain't a-goin' to find the gold. I'll git them first. Thet's my mission—to git Krafton Webber and his hellions, dead or alive. Wal, there ain't so many of his outfit living now. Just Webber and Texas Callahan and a breed."

"Yuh ain't forgettin' Jose?"

Jed smiled grimly.

"Thet feller ain't on my legal list, but I shore figger he's headin' for quick death."

And Jed Ryland would not listen to any further arguments about leaving Ezra. After a while the sheriff had to conserve his strength to enable him to hang on to the saddle-horn. They rode through the hilly country, heading across the land for Monument City. The ride would take all night.

They stopped after the first hour for Jed to tighten the bandage which bound Ezra's shirt against the wound. The sheriff dared not get down from the horse. He could only hope to sit grimly in the saddle, hanging on for hour after hour while the blood oozed from the wound.

Jed Ryland helped him to drink from a canteen. Then, with laboured breathing from Ezra Strang, the ride went on again. The horses plodded on at a walk, taking the flat trails through rocky outcrops, turning in the deep darkness of towering buttes.

"Them varmints—will—be headin' right—for thet gold now!" gasped Ezra. "Mebbe they think Rork Doonan took us!"

"They'll git a surprise—mebbe to-morrow!" said Jed grimly. "I aim to ride straight out after them."

"I reckon yuh don't like—sleeping—" panted Ezra Strang.

More than once Ezra lurched violently and Jed thought he was going to fall from the saddle. But the sheriff was iron-hard. The pain and loss of blood was sapping his strength, but sheer determination kept him doggedly in the leather.

The short night turned to pale light as sun-up approached. As blue fingers of light clawed into the sky, the two riders plodded steadily into the valley that gave on to Monument City. Never had ten miles seemed so long. Owing to Ezra's weak condition, they could not rowel the horses to a canter. As light chased away the night, they rode on and on, two weary mighty riders, one of whom was badly wounded.

They rode into the main street before the first folks were astir. Ezra grunted the location of the town's doctor. Jed rode on, one hand leading the sheriff's horse by the reins. Ezra Strang huddled and rolled in the saddle, sticking on grimly because he was a proud man and had willed himself to stay in leather to the end of the trail.

But in minutes Jed Ryland had aroused the doctor, and Ezra was taken over to his sheriff's office and laid in the bed. The skilled hands of the medical man took the blood-soaked bandage and shirt from the sheriff's back and side.

"Another inch an' this town would have needed a new sheriff!" barked the doc.

"They got a good sheriff now!"

drawled Jed. "What in heck would they want a new one for?"

Jed rolled two cigarettes and handed one to Ezra. Jed struck a match and helped his partner light up. Then Jed went to a nearby partition in the bedroom and found the big jug of water which stood there. He sluiced dust and sweat from him. In a minute he returned, said grimly to Ezra:

"Wal, I'm a-goin' to get me a fresh hoss out o' yore livery. Then I'm ridin' out. I'm takin' Winchester and two Colts."

"Yuh'll—kill—yuhself with—lack o' sleep!" grunted Ezra.

"I kin sleep in the saddle. Ever tried it, podner?"

"I figger I heerd thet afore!" barked Ezra.

"Wal, I'm a-goin'."

"Ain't yuh goin' to git a posse?"

"I don't need a posse. Those jiggers ain't got no guns. No, sirree, this is my last ride on Webber and his galoots and I figger to take it alone. Adios. But I'll be back."

"Yep. I reckon yuh'd better be back!" returned Ezra, and then he sank into a deep faint.

Jed Ryland knew the doctor could do everything for the sheriff. He had gotten to like the hombre during their association. He wanted him well again. He figured Ezra Strang would be sitting up when he rode back with Webber and his cohorts.

Jed was busy getting a fresh horse and some grub to fill his saddle-bag. Then, wasting very little time, he rode down the dusty street of false-fronted buildings. He smiled grimly as he realised the horse beneath him wanted to gallop.

He stopped only at Jean Marsh's caravan. She was busy already, polishing the brass.

"Howdy, Miss Jean!" he said gravely. "I wish I hadn't to ride out again, but I'm still after Krafton Webber. Thet feller is plumb lucky."

"I've been wondering about you!" she cried. "What's happened? Are you all right? You look tired."

"I aim to sleep in the saddle!" He grinned. "But I feel fine—now—after seeing yuh! Wal, I'll be ridin'. Next time I come back, Webber will be finished."

"When you ride back come along and tell me everything!" whispered the red-haired girl.

"I'll shore do that!" promised Jed with a sincere smile.

13

ADAY and a night had elapsed since the tangle with the law-men, when Rork Doonan had got his, and all the time Krafton Webber and his outfit had ridden on towards the Guadalupe Mountains. They had stopped only to water the horses and eat food themselves. They had given the animals very little time to crop at the sparse clumps of grass they found. And there had been little sleep for anyone.

But as sun-up clawed through the darkness, even Webber knew they had to stop and make camp. They just dared not push the horses any more. They were in desert country, with the terrible Guadalupes just ahead, rising majestically and dreadfully in endless peaks. No one knew when they would find the next water-hole. Maybe there was no water for miles. They had to think of the horses because without them they could perish in the arid land.

They had stopped at a water-hole only to find that the spot was simply a hole of hard-baked clay. There was no water.

Krafton Webber lurched down from the saddle. He could move only one hand. His shoulder was still stiff and sore. The wound was not mending too well because he had not given it a chance. He stood on the sand and stared over the endless waste. The land undulated with ridged, glaring gypsum sand. Then as a vast background the mountains loomed sheer from the badlands. They seemed very near, but Webber knew there was still some three hours riding over the desert. And with sun-up, the sand would become intensely hot.

Webber looked sneeringly at Jose Petrillio, still in his saddle.

"Wal, amigo, yuh figger to keep on ridin' to thet gold? Better git down off thet hoss afore the critter gits plumb tuckered fer good. Any man who breaks his hoss kin stay with the hoss. We'll want the spare for the gold."

They had got the reins of Rork Doonan's horse and taken it with them on the ride.

"I think we rest," said Jose Petrillio, and he slid off the saddle. He staggered as he stood on the desert. Webber watched him sway, and sneered.

"Yuh better take a nice long rest, amigo. Or mebbe yuh won't see no gold, huh?"

"I'll find the gold!" shrilled Jose Petrillio. Fatigue and hysteria were telling on him. "Why should we not find the gold? We have the map. You have half—and I have the other!"

"Keep it safe!" sneered Krafton Webber, his big cheeks caked with dust and sweat.

"I keep it safe!" shouted Jose Petrillio. "I want the gold! We all find gold, amigos! Do not fight, please! There will be plenty of gold for everybodees!"

"Aw, shut up about the blamed gold!" snarled Texas Callahan. "We ain't in thet hell-country yet! An' mebbe thar's a posse a-comin' this way!"

"Rork Doonan took care of those lawmen!" said Webber.

"Yuh only think he did!" sneered Texas.

The breed lay down in the shade of his horse's belly.

"I sleep!" he said. "Santa Maria, how I sleep! Tell me when you figger to ride, boss."

Krafton Webber squatted in the sand and pointed to the mountains.

"I reckon we'll sit hyar all day until it cools off, an' then we cross this last bit o' blamed desert. Should be a full moon tonight. We kin locate them twin peaks." Webber turned and looked meaningly at Jose Petrillio. "Then we got to put thet blamed map together, hombre. We got to start followin' the map. Cayn't do it if yuh got one half an' I got the other!"

"We can work together," said Jose Petrillio placatingly.

Krafton Webber lurched over to some

rocks which lay around the dried-up water-hole.

"I'm a-goin' to git some rest. We kin talk later. Give them hosses a feed from the fodder-bag somebody."

It was Texas Callahan who did the work. Webber lay with his back to the rocks, trying to get shelter from the rising sun. He was thinking, and his thoughts regarding Jose Petrillio were not pleasant.

The Mexican had tricked them and played around with them and still thought he could horn in for a share of the gold. Jose Petrillio was destined to receive a shock!

Krafton Webber smiled twistedly. He figured he could get the other half of the map from Jose Petrillio at any time. The party had no guns, but Texas and the breed would fall on Petrillio as soon as he gave the order.

Jose had played a tricky game. He had secreted a gun inside his pocket after making a deal to ride without weapons. They had got out of the jail so fast there had not been time to do anything but agree with the tricky hombre. Then when they were riding through the night, there had been a play to get the half of map from Jose, and the fellow had produced a gun and actually triggered off a shot to the sand!

Webber smiled again. He had talked through that little difficulty. They had ridden on again. The gun had been thrown to Rork Doonan.

Webber's lips parted in an angry snarl. If Doonan had got the two law-men in that gully, it was the best work the man had ever done. But it was impossible to guess what had happened. Certainly there had been some gun-fire. They had heard the shots as they rode furiously into the night.

Webber dozed in the shade of the rocks. Some time later when he became alert again he noticed how the sun had risen. The day was well into its swing now.

Krafton Webber did not move. He looked around through narrowed eyes that turned suspiciously without any movement of his head.

He saw that Jose Petrillio was sleeping. His horse was down on its belly, and the greaser was sitting against it.

Krafton Webber picked up a small pebble and threw it at Texas Callahan's face. The rannigan awoke with swift reaction. He coiled up and his hands went to the empty holsters. Then he stared at Krafton Webber.

The owl-hoot boss nodded the other to be silent. Webber rose and went over to the breed. He tapped the man's foot. The man came to life and stood up, staring with inquiring black eyes and ruthless, unshaven face.

"Git him!" sneered Webber. And then he nodded at Jose Petrillio.

The two outlaws pounced on the man. Jose Petrillio awoke to his danger. With a snarl of anger and fear, he thrust a hand inside his shirt.

As Texas Callahan and the breed held him down, a knife flashed in the Mexican's wildly moving arm.

But the man had little chance. While the breed held him down Texas Callahan twisted the knife hand until bones almost snapped. The knife fell to the sand. Krafton Webber picked it up.

"Yuh tricky devil! Yuh had a knife! Shore, yuh figgered to trick us! Wal, this is the end o' yore trail, amigo!"

The knife plunged down, turned in through the ribs and struck deep at the heart. Jose Petrillio gave a convulsive start. Blood spurted up to the knife hilt. Jose Petrillio whipped hands desperately to the knife as if he would pull it out of his body.

But death was overtaking him with huge strides. He screamed once and then choked into a rattle.

Krafton Webber went through the man's pockets with bloody hands. He found the piece of paper he wanted. He stuffed it into the pouch in his belt. Now he possessed the whole map again.

He tugged the knife free, and stood up, glaring savagely at the dying man.

"Wal, thet's the only thing yuh'll find

in this blamed desert—death, amigo! Haw, haw! Yuh figger we a-goin' to let yuh in on the gold? Yuh're a fool, Petrillio. Die, durn yuh! We're takin' yore hoss. Mebbe we'll need two critters to carry the gold!"

The crazy lust for gold had brought death to yet another man. Gold and death, the two were inseparable!

Webber glared over the stifling heat of the desert. The towering Guadalupes reared in endless jagged peaks as they had done for centuries.

"Cuss it, let's ride! I ain't campin' beside this coyote all day. Let the buzzards come alawng! We won't be hyar!"

They rode out of the place. They left a dead man lying beside a dried-up, clayey hole and some rocks. There was nothing else. Soon, when the riders had gone the buzzards would swoop out of the burning blue sky. The buzzards always knew. The black shapes seemed to arrive from nowhere.

But after half an hour of slow plodding

over the desert the intense heat seemed to knock all the strength out of the horses. The rest they had had was not enough. Grimly, Webber staggered down from his saddle and grabbed at his water canteen. He dribbled some water into his hand and let the horse suck it up before the heat evaporated it. Webber was no fool. Without the horse, they would never find another water-hole or get out of the dreaded country alive.

Some three hours later the three parched and choking men reached the first rise of broken hills. Webber studied the map, holding the portions together.

"See, thar's water hyar—the last to the bonanza. We got to ride another mile an' find thet water!"

They rode on, skirting the arid hill that rose right from the desert bed. They noted the points that checked with the map and were sure they would find the water-hole.

They found it a mile on as the map described. The hole was in the middle of a basin of rocks—but the water-hole was as dry as the one by which they had left the dead man!

Krafton Webber cursed Andrew Platt.

"Thet skunk ought to ha' put some directions about these water-holes on the map!"

"Thet blasted desert tramp knew all the tricks," Texas Callahan gasped. "He'd know when this blamed spring was in supply. He'd know the best seasons for making the trip."

"I wish we had thet old cuss with us!" grumbled Krafton Webber.

"Thet was the general idee," retorted Texas. "Only the old fool had to git himself a dose o' lead."

All at once the breed's horse collapsed. The breed stepped clear of the stirrups. He looked as if he wanted to kick the unfortunate animal, but he thought better of it. The horse just lay with belly to the ground and sagging head.

"We got to take thet long rest," said Webber grimly. "Mebbe we kin dig in thet hole and git a drop o' water. Might be water a bit down. We camp hyar."

Camp was simple. Men and horses looked for shade and sat down. But after an hour, during which the sun beat remorselessly against the rocks, the men realised there was work to do. They would have to try digging for water. They had some water in the canteens, but they simply dared not use it all up until they knew for certain that they could get a fresh supply.

They started digging with the tools they had snatched from Sheriff Jose Petrillio's office when they had raced off into the night.

But two hours of digging left them near exhaustion and with not a drop of water to show for their work. There was nothing but hard clay in the water-hole. It went all the way down.

Krafton Webber staggered away on the search for cholla cactus. Inside the big tough cactus plant there was water. True it had to be squeezed out drop by drop and caught in a pan. A man had to work hard to get even a few drops of water out of the cactus, but it was there and water was as valuable as gold.

Half an hour later the men had collected a few of the chunky cactus. Webber hacked one in half with Jose Petrillio's knife. He could not squeeze hard enough because of his injured shoulder. So he held a water canteen while Texas Callahan squeezed the hard, white plulp of the cactus. They watched the water drop in slow, precious globules. The breed was engaged on the same task. They knew it would take hours to fill a canteen.

But they had decided to spend the day resting and extracting water from the cholla cactus. They got half a canteen filled and then had to give it to the horses. Among five animals the water did not go far. Webber snarled.

"These critters are drinkin' as fast as we git the blamed water out o' these chunks of cactus!"

There was nothing for it but to work at squeezing the hard white meat of the plants. Drop by drop the canteen filled again, while the sun glared savagely and mockingly.

After some time, when the sun dropped from its midday height, they had to rest from the job of extracting water. They rationed out two inches of the sour water to each man. They hacked open a can of beans from the saddle-bag and ate them cold, drinking them down sparingly with the cactus water.

"We got to git a full canteen fer each man afore we start again!" choked Krafton Webber. "Even the blamed cholla don't grow up in them rocky slopes."

"I told yuh—nuthin' but rattlers," said Texas Callahan viciously.

"We got to git thet water collected, supposin' we stick hyar for two days!" rasped Webber. "There ain't another water-hole accordin' to the map. An' we might git away from the cholla."

The afternoon wore on, with the work of chopping the big cactus into handy chunks and then squeezing, squeezing patiently. The rocks around trapped the heat. The air was still and hot as an oven. Just to move brought rivulets of sweat on the men, caking the dust on their faces until it was a mask. Their tongues were parched and swollen, and they talked infrequently and then with effort.

Then hours later the sun reddened the desert horizon. Three silent, grim men sat with backs to rocks, staring over the desert. Behind them the land rose, first in foothills, and then to the mighty Guadalupes.

The three men had been sitting motionless for some time, tired of the task of extracting water from hard cactus, when Texas Callahan rose suddenly to his feet and pointed out over the desert.

"Thet's a man—on a hoss! It's him!"

They staggered up, stared unbelievably.

They saw the figure as a black shape on a tired horse. The setting sun was behind the rider. For a moment they thought it was a mirage, then they knew it was a rider, indeed. He was following their trail across the desert. He was heading right up to the spot where they were camped!

"Ryland, for shore!" swore Webber hoarsely.

His hands swung to empty holsters. He knew the saddle-boots held no rifle. Then his hands touched the knife. He slipped it inside his shirt, near where his belt tightened against his belly.

Slowly, the rider became larger, more detailed. They guessed it was Jed Ryland. They still could not recognise his features. He was still a long way off, a slowly moving speck.

"Ain't no good ridin' out!" snarled Webber. "Thet jigger would jest ride on and on after us. Guess he's got guns."

"He kin shoot us down!" snapped Texas.

"Yeah!" Webber took a violent drink from his canteen. Then he slung the bottle over the saddlehorn on his horse. He stood with his feet planted squarely apart. There was an expression of hate on his dust-masked face.

"Gawd, thet feller never lets up!"

snarled Texas. He laughed crazily. "Hell, he cayn't take us in! He'd never git us back to Monument City."

For long minutes they stared as if fascinated by the tired, slowly moving figure. All the time, Jed Ryland rode nearer and nearer.

"Thet feller must be as dead-beat as us!" choked Webber. "Wal, this is showdown. Git up behind them rocks and lie low," he snapped to the breed. "Yuh know what to do when yuh git a chance."

The breed scrambled around to some rocks and hid out of sight. Texas Callahan and Webber shifted until they were at one side of the rocks. They had one last trick to pull.

Even the outlaws' hardened nerves were frayed as they watched the weary rider top the rises of the undulating sands and then sink out of sight again. All the time Jed Ryland got nearer. Krafton Webber rasped at breath as the avenging man came on. There was something unbelievably implacable about the lone rider. It was impossible that he should have trailed them—but he had. They were facing grim reality and not a mirage.

And then Jed Ryland entered the flat, moved his weary horse through the strewn boulders that had rolled from the hills to the desert sands. In a minute more he was near enough for Webber and Texas to see the white mask of his face. They saw him sit tall in the saddle. Then they saw him slowly draw a gun from a holster. Another minute and he threw a leg over the horse's rump and slowly stood on the ground. Then he slowly walked forward, leading the animal. His gun was held waist-high.

Ten yards in front of the two outlaws he stopped.

"Whar's the breed?" he rasped.

"He's dead!" snapped Webber. "We buried him."

Jed Ryland swept his eyes over the horses. He noted there were five. Jed turned his startling blue eyes in a white sweat mask to the outlaws.

"I saw Jose Petrillio's body. The buzzards brought me up." Intense weariness slowed his words. "I aim to git yuh, Webber. Yuh, too, Texas. Yuh wanted men. Yuh're wanted for murder and robbery. Yuh got a map thet don't rightly belong to yuh."

"Yuh cayn't git us back to town!" sneered Webber. "Why, yuh're all in. I guess yuh ain't got no water for thet cayuse. An' there ain't no water in this hole. How'd yuh figger to take us back, Ryland?"

Jed walked away from his horse. He went about ten yards to the left. He was still pretty close to Krafton Webber and Texas Callahan.

"Yuh're lyin' about thet breed," he said slowly. "Yuh wouldn't bury him. It would be too much work. If he was dead yuh'd jest let the buzzards pick his bones."

"Yeah?" sneered Webber, but he grew tense. Not for a second did he take his eyes from Jed Ryland. He was wondering if he could throw a knife to beat a bullet.

"Yeah," said Jed Ryland, and then he made a surprising play.

He threw the Colt towards Krafton Webber. It fell about four yards from the outlaw. It lay in the sand, and Webber stared fixedly at it.

Jed drew his other Colt. He held it loosely, barrel pointing at the ground.

"I figger yuh're right, Webber. I cayn't take yuh across thet badland—not the two o' yuh and the breed, wherever he is hidin'. But I offer yuh a chance. Yuh or Texas. Yuh kin choose. There's a gun on the ground. One of yuh go for it. I guarantee it's loaded. If yuh kin beat me, I reckon I'll be buzzard bait instead o' you. If one o' yuh go for the gun and fail, the other jigger can take the chance. I'll holster my hogleg."

There was dead silence. Neither Webber nor Texas moved. The gun lay on the sand tantalisingly near and yet dangerously far away.

"We ain't makin' the play!" snarled Webber. "I git yore idee. Yuh figger to shoot afore a feller ever touches the gun! Yuh ain't given anything away."

"I'll go for a gun when a feller touches the Colt and not afore," said Jed quietly.

Again there was silence.

"It's a trick!" rasped Webber's hoarse voice.

"Maybe yuh'd like me to gun yuh down right now?" said Jed.

Texas Callahan moved slowly forward. He stepped one yard then crouched. He moved another yard and sank even lower to the sand. All the time he stared glaringly at Jed Ryland. His black eyes glinted against the caking mask of dust and sweat. He slithered nearer to the gun, and his breath was rasping.

For a few seconds he crouched still beside the gun, fingers merely inches from it. His face twisted under the dust as he tensed himself for the final movement.

"Yuh ain't a-goin' to git me, Ryland! I'll take yuh with me if I'm lucky! Thar ain't goin' to be no gold for anybody, I reckon. It's—death—fer—everybody!"

He snatched at the Colt, scooped it up desperately with all his border experience at handling a gun. He triggered.

Jed Ryland threw off tiredness in a flash of unbelievable speed. He clawed and produced the gun in magical swiftness. Two guns roared at once.

But other things happened. A knife hurtled through the air with a vicious hissing sound. The blade scraped past Jed's neck, tearing skin and sinew.

A rock flew at the Texas Ranger, thrown by the breed.

Jed dodged the rock desperately.

His bullet had killed Texas Callahan as the other had fired. As a result, the outlaw's aim had jolted. The slug cut air above Jed's head. Texas Callahan had had every chance and had been beaten.

Jed Ryland clamped a hand to his neck and felt blood. All at once the breed threw another rock. As it rose in the air Jed Ryland drew bead on the outlaw.

Crack!

The shot took the breed in the chest and he staggered back to thud against the rocks and die.

Jed Ryland jumped swiftly to evade the flying rock. As it thudded to the sand Jed ran to get the gun which lay beside Texas Callahan. He picked it up. He walked away a few steps, his eyes on the desperate Krafton Webber.

"Yuh an' me now, Webber!" he mocked. "What price gold, hombre?"

"If yuh figger to kill, git on with it!" hissed the man.

"I'm givin' yuh a chance," grated Jed Ryland. "Ride back as prisoner or pick up this gun!"

And Jed threw the gun he had picked up to Webber's feet. The Colt hit the sand only a foot from Krafton Webber. The big man stared down with gaunt lines tight on the fantastic mask of dust and sweat.

Jed put his gun back in the right-hand holster.

"Yuh got a chance," he rasped. "An' thet's more'n yuh ever gave anybody. What's it to be? Yuh goin' to walk to yore hoss or go for the gun?"

Krafton Webber had lived by Colt fire for years. He had been ruthless and confident. All this added up to guts of a kind.

He did not dive for the gun. He sank slowly, grimly, his red-rimmed eyes fixed on Jed Ryland. Then his hand groped for the gun. Jed stood immobile, tight-lipped, his hands dangling near his holsters. He had one gun. He would need only one gun—or he would never need another.

Krafton Webber whipped the Colt up and fired.

Jed threw his gun with a speed which beat the other's movement. Jed's gun exploded first.

Webber fell backwards and put a tilt on the gun even as it roared. The slug tore a hole in the sky. But another slug had ripped into the outlaw's chest, shattering sinew and bone.

Slowly, with a contortion of white-caked face, the man died and lay still.

Jed Ryland went over slowly and fumbled in the pockets of the man's shirt.

He found the intact map in the belt pouch.

Jed rose. He hardly looked at the map which had caused so much blood. He stared at the eternal Guadalupes, arid and dreadful peaks and canyons. He was thinking other men would risk their lives to seek the gold. There would always be a lure where there was gold.

But for him there was the trip back to Monument City to see a feller named Ezra Strang and a gal called Jean Marsh. He wanted to see how Ezra was making out; and he wanted to just speak and spend some time with Jean.

He did not know why, but it all just seemed more important than gold.

An hour later, with a bandage around his neck, he rode out over the desert. The other horses came along on a lead rope. He had gathered the water which the outlaws had collected. With sundown, the night was cooler now.

He felt mighty weary, but he knew he would make the journey all right. He would get back to make a report. He

would get back because he had plenty to
live for and the way he intended to live
was GOOD.

THE END